SANJA

CABIN IN THE WOODS

NOVAK

Cabin in the Woods

ISBN: 979-8-9907392-0-8

ISBN (eBook): 979-8-9907392-1-5

ANG Publishing

For Matt,

Who life wouldn't be the same without.

CHAPTER ONE

Whenever it starts to snow, I think about a cold, dark place in the middle of the woods. Where slivers of moonlight show the way. Where the fog makes its way around and through the trees. My mind wanders to his face when he told me. The surprise and fear I felt. He never looked at me that way in all the years I had known him. His blue eyes glistened, looking grey in the dim moonlight. The cold we felt, lessened by the heat between us. Each of my senses were intensified. Listening, feeling, and looking for something, anything, in the distance, but left wanting. I worried that even if I had heard a sound, it would only be an illusion, nothing concrete to pull us out of this cold, dark place.

My imagination runs wild. Was this it? Would we ever escape? It felt like hours had passed already waiting in the deep thickness of these woods. The cliff below us, steep, limiting our movements. How would anyone ever find us—that is if anyone ever comes to look.

The night swallows any remaining light. It is very possible we may never get out of this alive.

CHAPTER TWO

To: ElvaBronson@gmail.com

From: CalistaJokovic@gmail.com

Subject: Holiday

Hi! It's me. I know it's been a while, but I can't wait to see you! Do you plan on leaving early in the morning tomorrow? I know it will be a bit of a drive. Let me know if you and Tom will be driving together. Maybe we can follow each other? Tina mentioned the ride would be about 6 or so hours depending on traffic. I'm hoping for less, but I'm not the best of drivers, especially around the mountains. I can't remember the last holiday I took in the mountains. I wonder if Tina will bring Anthony, she seems to be avoiding the question. Let's hope it's an easy and relaxing one, we can all use it, I'm sure. Anyway, looking forward to catching up with you guys and relaxing with a glass of wine by the fire. Let me know your plans.

XO,

Cal

I shut my laptop thinking about Elva. I can't remember the last time I saw her. Must have been at least a year or more ago. Time flew by so quickly these last few years, especially with the pandemic looming over us for longer than we could have been prepared for. Everyone seems to have changed since it started. Probably made most of us a bit more introverted. It's hard to believe it was possible we would drift this far apart when we were so close. When Tina invited us to come out to the mountains, I thought of a million reasons why I couldn't make it, but the truth was that all of those reasons were only excuses. I was avoiding them. Perhaps this trip will bring us back together, make us closer like we used to be. Some of us got married and had children, others explored the world. Some continued to work in offices while others worked remotely from home. Some switched or quit jobs to start something new and exciting. Some of us were too afraid to leave the house for a while. Online sales were peaking. I wish I had been creative and taken advantage of that, but I was never crafty enough.

I definitely felt a change in the times. I managed to get away from my nine-to-five job and started working from home. It helped pay the bills and I'd hated driving to work every day. I became a homebody and still managed to make money from it.

Pulling out a gray spiral notebook from my desk drawer, I began to make a list of all the things I needed to bring on the trip. I am far too Type "A" to pack anything without a list. Not sure if some of my clothes even fit—my wardrobe since transitioning to home consisted of joggers, tank tops, and house slippers. The occasional blazer was worn when needed for my *Zoom* meetings, but that was definitely not something I needed for this kind of trip. I felt comfortable knowing that the joggers stacked neatly on top of my dresser would be the most important things to bring aside from my hiking boots and my three-in-one jacket. It was good for the rain, wind and all that jazz.

I have a short but fit frame. Tina and Elva tower over me at their stature of five foot seven to five foot ten. I am a comfortable five foot three. I'm bustier than Elva and Tina although last I heard Elva had "enhanced" herself.

I scoop my dark blonde hair off my face and catch myself in the mirror. I look so tired. I used to have luscious long flowing heavily highlighted blonde hair throughout my entire life until just after my law school graduation. I chopped most of it off to a mid-length and dyed it dark brown. I wanted to be taken seriously and I had managed to do so. But I realized it just wasn't me, so I decided to lighten it up again. It looks much better on my semi-pale European complexion. But still as I study at my reflection in the mirror—I can't help but to only see my flaws. My green eyes are now sunken in. They look worn out and tired. Not the bright eyed and bushy tailed girl I once was. I look closer tracing the dark circles underneath my eyes trying to conceal the darkness with a few daps of concealer, but it can only do so much. Frustrated, I throw the conceal to the side. I need a break to regroup.

I decided on minimal luggage, my favorite carry-on bag. It was big enough for the basics and divided enough to separate everything. I tend to roll my clothes, a technique I picked up from *Pinterest,* since rolling allows for more of my things to fit in this small bag and God knows I need more space for all the things I intend to bring. I pat myself on the back for discovering this method and start rolling. I'm sure we will just sit around in the cabin, play some games and catch up. I mean, what else could we do in the middle of nowhere?

My attention shifts back to Elva. What has she been up to? We used to talk every day. Then every day turned into every two days, then every week, then once a month, then every two months. Elva moved into the city and the frequency of when we saw each other became less and less. We texted all the time, but life got in the way of actually talking.

We were only kids when we met, Elva and me. She was the best friend a girl could ask for. She helped me get a locker in the north hall that was only for seniors when I was still a sophomore. She could convince you to do anything, and always got what she wanted. I liked her because she was silly and beautiful at the same time. We tried to take every class together. The only class she wouldn't take with me was weightlifting. She thought I was taking it just to scope out the boys. Truthfully, I didn't have the guts to flirt with anyone. I took the class for the free credits. I was always about the easy A even though I didn't suffer academically. I needed some activity classes to show I was involved and not a complete nerd but wouldn't drag down my GPA. I planned to go to law school and needed my transcripts to be in good shape and show how well rounded I was.

Elva was involved in drama and theater throughout high school. She was a right-brainer kind of girl. Liked the arts, liked to be the center of attention, but not in a self-centered way. She didn't have the grades, but she managed to fly through with her bright personality. Everyone liked her, there was nothing not to like about her.

When her mother passed in early college, it changed her completely. She became more introverted, more school orientated, and took college seriously. Something about fulfilling her mother's dreams. She pushed forward and really excelled in college, which paid off throughout the rest of her life. Her grades earned her scholarships and the internship of her dreams at Top Fashion. She became Director of Fashion basically right out of college after her internship ended and her career only skyrocketed from there.

*****

The clock struck half-passed ten and I realize I haven't finished packing. It's only a four-day trip and since Monday's a holiday so I was only taking one day off. Truthfully, I could probably work from anywhere with decent WIFI, but I needed the time off to take a breath, get out of the house, regroup, reconnect with people again.

My smartwatch pings to notify me of a new email. That was quite quick.

To: CalistaJokovic@gmail.com

From: ElvaBronson@gmail.com

Subject: RE: Holiday

Cal! Hey love, can't wait to see you too! We are packed and ready to rock and roll. We will be up and ready at 5:00 am, hope your bags are packed! Tom is driving and he wants to get ahead of the work crowd, get on the road early. We should arrive around the early afternoon. You are welcome to drive up with us if you want instead, no need to follow us. We can pick you up. We're staying over at granny's house so if we leave an hour early, we should have enough time to pick you up and still make it up by 2:00 pm or so... Let me know.

XO,

Elva

My luggage is bursting at the seams, at this point I am only able to zip it up while sitting on it.

I hit reply from my smartwatch:

To: ElvaBronson@gmail.com

From: CalistaJokovic@gmail.com

Subject: RE:RE:Holiday

Perfect, I'll be ready and waiting for you outside. Thanks, so much girl—I appreciate the ride. Much more fun traveling together. See you tomorrow morning.

Cal

I'm relieved to not have to drive tomorrow.

***

The alarm clock sounds bright and early at 4:15 am. I never wake up this early, but, let's be honest, they are doing me a huge favor by picking me up since I *hate* driving. Elva's grandmother lives in a neighboring city, about forty-five minutes from my townhouse, so I have a little bit of time to get myself together if I get moving immediately.

The grinder to my automatic coffee maker goes off like a bang. Every time I hear it, I get excited. I have been a coffee fiend since college. I don't know how people who don't drink coffee wake up in the morning, I would be completely useless without it. I shuffle my way over to the coffee maker and stand there as if staring at it will somehow make the brew drip faster. I open the cabinet above it and pull out my favorite mug. It's a basic-looking white mug with a picture of the mountains of Jahorina in Bosnia. I bought it on my first trip there to ski with my family. The mug was just the right size for the amount of coffee I generally ingest, and I made sure to use and abuse it each day.

I look outside to see if any cars are out in front of my townhouse. It's so dark outside it still feels like the middle of the night.

It's about 5:00 am when I make my way out the front door. I don't see Elva and Tom yet, so I grab a second steaming cup of joe and sit out on the porch swing. A chill travels through me. The winter months are approaching although it's a bit more uncomfortable than usual for the time of year. The fall has always brought in the wind, especially since my street is curved and creates a wind tunnel. I grab a scarf to drape over my shoulders and my neck. Much better.

I think about how nice it will be for all of us to get together again. I'm anxious since I haven't kept up with them as much as I would have liked. I used to be so extroverted, always looking for my next outing, but COVID really made me take a major step back. I became more of a homebody, enjoying the silence around me when I didn't have to listen to screaming clients most of the workday. It'll be fine. I mean, what's the worst that could happen, right?

I appreciated Tina organizing the trip. If she hadn't, I don't think any of us would have gone the distance to put in the effort to plan it out. Tina's great aunt left her a cabin when she passed away a few years ago. It was quite an inheritance. She had been a very wealthy women whose family owned land in the Berkshires back in the day before the Berkshires were the Berkshires. Her great aunt never had any children of her own, so she always treated Tina and her brother like her own children. Spoiled them endlessly. Tina was lucky to have her, and, in her great aunt's late years, she was lucky to have Tina. Tina cared for her like she was her mother.

Tina's father was killed in a head-on collision about ten or so years back. Tina was devastated, she never got passed it. Aunt Millie never cared much for their mother and made it a point to remove her any type of inheritance. She made sure that Tina and Joe shared the inheritance should anything happen to their father. Tina split the inheritance with her brother, Joe, who could have cared less for Millie or their father. It was a surprise to the rest of the family that Joe wasn't excluded from the inheritance, but Aunt Millie wouldn't do that to him. She loved them both equally.

Joe was a bit of a loner, not in a quiet way, but more in the way that he distanced himself from the family. He moved away right after graduating high school. He'd had a tumultuous relationship with his mother and an even worse one with his father. His father's rules chafed against his rebellious nature. Their mother was shocked when he applied for college. But it made sense. Joe was smart, passing the SATs with a breeze, scoring high enough to pick anywhere he wanted to go to school. I guess he realized living on the road with his guitar may not be enough to get by, especially when he blew through most of his inheritance in short order.

I met Tina and Joe in college at the University of Pittsburgh. Well, it was Tina that attended college there. She was studying engineering. Tina and I were roommates, assigned at random. I spent four years in the same dorm with her even though I was pre-law. Tina and I got along well and became fast friends. It took a bit of finagling to stay in a dorm room with her since we were on different major tracks, but I made it happen. I just had to start early or run to my classes to get to them in time since my classes were located on the other end of campus.

Tina was a great roommate. Clean, courteous, and quiet. Kept to herself most of the time. Liked to read and talk about her projects. She spent a lot of her time in our dorm room putting together a plan to build her first robotic widget that served us coffee in the morning and tea in the afternoon. She named him "Gizmo," he was our robotic butler. He was fantastic. She had the mind of a true scientist, programmer, and engineer.

I tried to pull her out of her comfort zone as much as possible. I recall begging her to join the intramural tennis team on campus. "Cal, I can't..." she would say, but I knew that "can't" meant "she didn't want to." She was comfortable being alone and preferred to stay in, read a book, watch a movie, build her next "Gizmo."

As much time as she liked to spend alone, she also spent with me. She made me laugh so hard I would literally pee my pants. It's the part of her anyone but me rarely saw. She was witty, sharp, and hilarious. We shared everything with each other. We kept no secrets from each other. There wasn't a topic that was ever off limits. We became as close as sisters, mimicking each other's laugh and thoughts. We were best friends.

I knew that Elva was jealous of our relationship. We got close so quickly. I would call her and tell her all about Tina. "Ah-huh" she would say to basically everything I said showing little interest in how much fun I was having without her. But then Elva came around. She visited from New York and stayed with Tina and I in our dorm room. Tina eventually grew on her.

When Elva came to visit us at PITT the three of us would go out into town. Elva loved going to nightclubs, but we'd remind her we weren't in New York City, we didn't really have nightclubs out here. Sure, our town had "clubs"—but they were more like pubs with a DJ. Tina went along once we pushed her into going out and managed to have a good time.

"You're definitely funny" Elva would say to Tina, who was excited she receive the compliment, but then Elva would add "...funny looking" and crack herself up. Elva was a jokester. It would piss Tina off, but she kept her composure and her mouth shut.

The two of them would get into a pissing match, but then end up hugging it out in the end. Eventually, we became like three sisters. You don't always get along with your sisters, but you love them and always have their back.

Tina wasn't much of a partier, but I think that our living dynamic pushed her out of her comfort zone, and she ultimately enjoyed going out and spending time together. We had some of the best campus parties. Those engineers knew how to study hard and play harder. I'll never forget freshman year when we attended Greek Night on campus. It was a night when eligible and interested students were invited to the Greek houses on campus and introduced to Greek Life. There were about fifteen different sororities and fraternities on campus. All houses were open for eligible recruits that night with each of the houses lined up, side by side, looking for newbies to join. The invited students would essentially "walk the Greek line" and be bombarded by fliers, whistles, and drinks as they passed each house in hope they would drop in and sign up to pledge. What it actually felt like was walking from one party to the next while members attempted to lure us in. I knew nothing about Greek life, nor did I want any part in it, but the attention was exciting.

That was the same night I met Joe. He was a bit older than Tina. He was visiting from Central Florida where he went to a larger college mid-state. He'd dragged out his first two years as a freshman until he learned financial aid wouldn't pay for his extended stay if he didn't graduate in a timely fashion. Perhaps he was trying to keep the school's reputation as the university that "you can't finish." His fraternity was hosting a travel meet-and-greet to enroll brothers transferring to the University of Pennsylvania. He volunteered since his younger sister was enrolled. Joe was a tall, semi-sporty built and with dark features. His hair was short, but curly dark brown hair, large round blue eyes, and about six foot two. I remember thinking he looked like Adrian Grenier from *Entourage,* but taller and more fit. You could tell right off the bat that he was witty and smart. Girls swooned when he played guitar, and he could keep anyone hooked with an engaging story.

Then there is Anthony, Tina's boyfriend who she started dating about a year ago or so. She told me a little about him right after they met. She was stunned when he asked for her number, giddy like a child. She wasn't used to the attention. They met at a bar. The early college years Tina wouldn't have stepped foot in a bar without being pushed into it. She was in downtown Manhattan for a work event and that's when she first laid eyes on him. Afterwards, she gushed about how handsome he is—so tall and slender with a dark Mediterranean complexion. She was all lust at first sight. He literally swept her off her feet. Wine and dined her and took her to Broadway shows in the city. He earned a spot in her heart quickly.

"He gave me a key to his apartment" she texted. That was fast, but I was happy for her.

She had a thing for Italian men and a burning desire to visit Italy. When she found out that his extended family lives in Rome, that was the icing on the cake.

"Gusmano" she texted, that's his last name. He has a big family—she always wanted a big family. With the loss of her father and Aunt Millie, she only had her mother and brother who she isn't close with and rarely speaks to either one.

She'd say, "I want stability." Her messages came hit me as *hopeful* that Anthony would give her that and so much more.

Shortly after that Tina became preoccupied and stopped texting me. Her world became all about "Anthony." I was in over my head with work, so I didn't think much about the silence between us, but as time passed, we lost touch. I'd like to get to know him better.

***

I haven't dated, like really dated someone, since after high school. It sounds pathetic, but don't feel too bad for me—I went on a few dates, but never found someone that stuck out enough to call "my boyfriend."

I spent most of my time dreaming of becoming a lawyer, studying for the LSATs and passing the bar exam. I didn't feel the need to spend my time concentrating on a meaningless relationship with someone I would eventually dump.

I am an excellent singer, but my audience consists of my cat, Mr. Whiskers. He's my biggest fan. I play tennis with Jerry's sister, Adele, every third weekend. She's sporty and loves to compete. She helps me break a sweat and I certainly return the favor, but we don't spend much time together socially off the tennis court. On rare occasions, we share a cup of coffee together here and there, but other than that we never hang out. I work a lot and spend the majority of my free time alone reading for pleasure. My life has become very monotonous.

I spent most of my childhood in Pennsylvania living in the small town of Bellefonte, where I grew up. I left for college, went to PITT, then stayed after graduation to attend law school. The drive from PITT back home wasn't so bad, about three hours, which allowed me to visit my mom as often as I could.

I had big dreams to move to New York City like Elva and Tina did, but right after my law school graduation I made my way back to Bellefonte and never left. I stayed because I landed my first job with Jerry almost immediately upon moving home. In fact, I didn't receive my bar passage results yet from the State of Pennsylvania when Jerry offered me a job at his law firm. I grabbed it immediately. I knew I needed to start paying off my student loans ASAP and Jerry was my immediate lifeline. He took a risk on me that paid off. Plus, I was able to move out on my own and pay rent without my mom's help.

"Meowww..."

Mr. Whiskers rubs his soft black and white torso along the side of my calf, breaking my thoughts. My hand runs from the top of his silky head to his long curvy tail as he passes. He is going to miss me. I admire Mr. Whiskers' enthusiasm each day. He's happy with his routine. He scales the townhouses' windowpanes, knocks the ball around in his kitty jungle gym, gets pet and treats whenever he asks. *Meow*—he's happy—I wish I could say the same.

I take a sip of my coffee—it's no longer warm. I rest the mug on the wicker table beside my rocking chair.

A change of scenery would help clear my head. I'm looking forward to getting away from this repetitious life—even if that means just for a long weekend away.

CHAPTER THREE

Not a minute past 5:10 am, I see headlights approaching as a car comes around the bend. It's a silver sedan. As it gets closer, I see the very distinctive Jaguar hood ornament and realize it's Elva. The car pulls swiftly into my driveway, and she jumps out.

"Darling! Where have you been my whole life?" she says jokingly as she runs over and embraces me. "We haven't' seen each other in what? A year, two? How did we let the time get away from us?" she says smiling and hugging me again.

Elva had gone off to become a mega success and left our small town. I would have done the same thing if I didn't feel a sense of loyalty to Jerry, who I'd worked for since I graduated law school. Jerry runs a small firm just outside of Hershey. During and after COVID he's been gracious to allow me to continue working remotely. He's become like family to me. I always liked and respected him. I couldn't just leave him behind. He was aging and I don't think his weak heart could handle another hit after his second wife left him and he survived his third heart attack. He knew that he could rely on me to take care of his long-term clients, since I had inherited their problems while he was out on medical leave. All the clients were just about as old or older than Jerry, each of whom had a child they wished to disinherit every other month. The problem with Jerry is he had a "handshake policy" on billing that didn't allow us to collect payment as quickly as I would have liked. Sometimes the clients even died before we got payment. Jerry seemed to be okay with that. He's honest and friendly, but a terrible businessman.

"In the flesh, Mrs. Elva Bronson, top-of-the-line chick! Where have you been, hun?" I yelled as I embraced her back. I really missed her, she is the same as she was when I last saw her just a bit older, but aging looked good on her.

"Ready to hit the road? Where are your bags?" she asks with an expression of confusion looking past the one small piece of luggage I have sitting on my porch.

"That's it, just this one for me." I say.

"You are better than me, my friend," she says as she points over to the backseat of the Jaguar filled with Louis Vuitton and Gucci bags stacked neatly on top of each other.

"How did you get Tom in the car?" I say, laughing as I wave over to Tom who is sitting a bit too close to the steering wheel in the driver's seat. You could tell the bags stacked behind him were pressing against his lower back by the expression on his face, though he doesn't seem to mind. He knows how Elva always overpacks. Whether she's traveling for one day or twenty, the girl needs her stuff.

Tom waves back enthusiastically from the driver's seat.

From what I remember about Tom, he's a patient man. You have to be with Elva. She talks a mile a minute and has no problem speaking her mind. Tom is quiet and, at times, somewhat mysterious. In the five years they have been together, I may have heard him argue once and it was about something silly like whether his coffee was caffeinated or decaffeinated. He never seemed to ever contest anything Elva did or said. Maybe he just never had a reason to doubt her.

Tom made his money in investments. He met Elva at a club while on a business trip in Cincinnati, Ohio. Elva was there directing a group of women advertising a winter fashion line with a roaring twenties aesthetic. She reserved the location for the event specifically because it was in an old underground tunnel and had a speakeasy vibe. The name *Elva Bronson* brought hype to the event. Everyone wanted to have a sneak peek at her new collection, but not everyone got an opportunity because she made sure it was private. It made the event more exclusive.

She was wearing a nude, long-sleeved bodysuit completely made of crystals, and leggings. Her body was fit and tight, and she wore it like she knew what she was doing and that was selling that outfit and herself to the investors who flocked to the event. She wore her hair down with a shimmering cap that of crystals and nude lace. The head piece was right out of the *Gatsby* movie. The rest of her hair flowed down to her waist in a rich auburn color, lusciously wavy. I remember her looking like a goddess.

I never had her type of appeal. She was mesmerizing and she knew it. At times I was surprised we were friends. I knew I was only there because I was her best friend otherwise. I definitely did not belong. The room was filled with people just as beautiful as her. My fit but short frame would never make its way into a one-piece like hers. My mid-length dark-blonde hair would never achieve the same volume. I wasn't there to be like her, but I would be lying if I said I didn't want to be her at times. I was excited I was invited to her private event. I was always her biggest cheerleader, and I didn't mind getting out of town for a few days to support her. Cincinnati was a short flight from Pennsylvania, and I needed a break.

When she approached Tom for the first time, I knew he would have sold his last kidney to have Elva and she knew it. Tom was a stocky man. Short physic, not likely over five foot eight inches. Short dark brown hair, a neatly shaped crew cut, well dressed, and a nice friendly smile. Elva would never have noticed him, but his wealth certainly helped attract her. He ate from the palm of her hand. She cared more about his deep pockets, and he knew it, but he didn't seem to care. That night was a great success for Elva, as usual. She sold out and had back orders amounting to a year's salary in one night. She made sure that Tom was one of the investors.

I saw the way Tom looked at her, like she was golden. You could see the obsession in his eyes the moment she spoke to him. Before the nights' end, I walked into a small alley way underneath the bar looking for the restrooms and caught Tom with his pants undone thrusting into Elva as she laid on top of a small wine rack below the stairs. She turned her head, catching my eye. I was so embarrassed, but I realized she wasn't. She gave me a wink and carried on by grabbing his thick muscular thighs, pulling him closer to her. I realized then she knew what she was doing. She made sure she got him, all of him. She didn't need his money. Her reputation exceeded his on any given day, but she could make use of his family name in the fashion industry. She wanted to secure his investments in her and her alone, so she did what she had to do.

***

I grabbed my bag, shifting it to the side to make space in the small trunk of the Jaguar.

"Ready to go?" Elva asks as I secure the truck.

"Let's do this!" I climb into the back passenger seat of the car. I rest my arm securely on top of three of her bags so that they wouldn't topple over on me while we drove.

"Are you okay back there? I know there isn't too much space. Tom put his bags in the trunk somehow and I got the back seat," she laughs.

Of course she did. Tom would have left his bags at home just so she could fit hers in the car. Luckily, he managed to get one in.

"All set" I say semi-enthusiastically. I can already see this is going to be a long, uncomfortable drive into the mountains.

I must have drifted off because I suddenly wake up. We are still on the road. I look out the window and see only trees around us. I look over at Tom in the driver's seat, holding a large tumbler in his right hand and gripping the steering wheel with his left. He's humming a familiar tune, but I can't quite it make out. I look over at Elva. She's talking on speakerphone while putting on lipstick at the same time.

"I told you that I was out of town for a few days. No, I am not going to come by today. Call El Moris, he will give you the samples of the new line. I cannot even leave for a minute without all of you idiots losing your way. No, no, no, FIND A WAY!" she yells and disconnects the call.

Another day in paradise.

Elva catches my eye in her phone's reflection and turns around. "Hey! There you are sleepy head. We are about an hour away. You have been passed out," she says.

I rub my eyes, "I see you brought your work with you… planning to turn the car around?" I say half-jokingly as I have no clue who she was talking to or what on earth it was about. I know how obsessed she is with her job.

She scoffs. "Those morons can't do anything without me. I get away from them for a minute and they fall apart."

What would anyone do without her, I think. Knowing Elva my entire life, she always has a problem and it's never one she couldn't fix. I just wonder how Tom can be so calm next to her while she's yelling on the phone right next to his ear.

"Mmmhhmmmm… hmmmm…" Tom continues to hum. He isn't listening to either one of us. He's got his earbuds in. Hopefully he can still hear a car horn or sirens, but I'm not sure. Tom makes his way off the highway to a gas station.

"Make sure to grab me the Ultralights," Elva says as she blows Tom an air kiss. Tom gets out of the car and pretends to catch the air kiss from Elva's lips. How sweet.

"Want anything Cal?" he asks me.

"Sure, I'll take a Coke," I say as I dig into my purse and hand him a ten-dollar bill.

"Your money is no good here," he says smiling and walks into the small but well-lit convenience store in front of the pump.

"He's so sweet," I say.

Elva is still using her phone as a mirror, this time to put on liquid eyeliner.

"Uh huh, he's alright." She turns toward me and adds, "You know I wouldn't have to work a day in my life if it was up to him. He would just have me sit at home in heels and a mini skirt. I think he forgets sometimes who he married." She frowns. I could sense a bit of animosity in her voice.

"I'm sure he just wants you to be happy," I say.

"You know, when I had Flora, he begged me to stop working, to stay home with her. He wanted to make sure I was with her constantly," she says. "I told him I would never quit because I have an empire to run for God sakes! He doesn't get it." She sighs.

Flora is Elva and Tom's four-year-old daughter. She is currently being catered to by nannies and Elva's mother-in-law, who has employed her own nannies for when Flora is in her care. Something about the way Elva talks about Tom makes me uncomfortable.

"So how are you these days, Cal? I've been keeping up with you on Instagram, but there's not too many posts lately. Whatcha' been up to?" she asks, changing the subject and her vibe.

"Not too much excitement in my world, just been working, holding down the fort," I say.

"Is that old man still up and running?" She is referring to Jerry. She didn't think I should have stayed working for him after the first year when I had the opportunity to move to the city for a job opportunity with a big name firm.

"He's doing well. He's in and out of the hospital so I've been running the show for quite some time," I say.

"I don't know why you take that shit. He doesn't pay you nearly half of what you are worth. You graduated magna cum laude from PITT's law school and you're still dragging ass with Jerry." She shakes her head.

I'm sure she can see the dismay in my expression, but I bite my tongue. We don't all have daddy's money to start up a brand or a guy like Tom to fund any deficits. I had to work hard for everything I achieved and pay my own way through it.

My mother was a seamstress and my father a business developer. When he passed away when I was young, my mother was left with taking care of me and a load of debt he hadn't told her about. She sewed one dress at a time for the well to dos. When he passed away, the lights went out, figuratively and literally. I helped my mother with her business, since she only worked part time initially, but then gradually gained full-time employment in a larger boutique downtown. There was plenty of work hemming high-end wedding dresses. After about two years, she was up and running a full-time business and the lights were no longer off.

***

Tom returns to the car and hands me a Pepsi. "Sorry it's all they had" he says.

He gives a box of Carpi Ultralights to Elva. "Here you go darling. Don't let the fucking stuff kill you."

His tone strikes me as odd, as if he is joking, but not entirely. There is definitely some animosity there.

Elva rolls her eyes as she rolls down the window and ignites an Ultralight.

CHAPTER FOUR

At half past twelve, the sun finally shines through the clouds as we approach a narrow, but long driveway. We drive up the hill following the gravel road, arriving at a grand structure that could only technically be called a log cabin. The two-story structure is surrounded by tall pine trees. I step out of the Jag, taking a long, deep breath of the fresh air. Between Elva's cigarettes and the conversation, I needed it.

There is a small carved wooden bear beside the doorway holding a tray. As I approach, I see there is a sealed envelope on the tray. I pick up the envelope and hold it up to the light.

"Well, just open it won't you!" Elva's voice breaks my silent curiosity.

There's nothing written on the exterior of the envelope, nothing to indicate who it's addressed to.

"Will you just open the damn thing?" she yells again, this time with more impatience.

"All right, all right. You need to chill woman. I was just looking to see if I could figure out who it's addressed to since it doesn't have anything written on the outside."

"I'll just do it then," she says, snatching the envelope out of my hands and opening it.

It always has to go her way, doesn't it? I roll my eyes.

Elva reads its contents out loud.

"ATTENTION GUESTS—Please be mindful of your head walking in and out of the rooms. Please do not feed the wildlife. Do not leave trash out at night, it will be a mess come the morning. The entry key is in a secure place, located behind the wooden bear. The code to open the lock housing the key has been sent to the primary guest, i.e. the one who booked the cabin. In case of emergency call 888-234-9987 and ask for Carla. Enjoy your stay."

"Great, where the hell is Tina? Do we seriously have to sit outside of this place and wait until they get here to open the door?" Elva huffs.

"I can give her a call and see how far out she is," I say. "Surely she's close." Although I have no idea where Tina is, I don't want to hear Elva complain.

I take out my phone from my crossbody bag and dial Tina's number.

"Hello?"

"Hey! It's Cal, we made it to the cabin and its GORG…" Who am I talking like this? "… Anyway, we opened the envelope. It says you have a code or something to get the key out of the lock?"

"Oh right, right. I forgot the manager resets that. Let me give her a call. I didn't get a text. Call you back," Tina says and hangs up.

"So, what's the verdict?" Elva pushes.

"Tina has to call for the code and she'll call us back," I say.

Elva rolls her eyes hard enough they should have made a sound.

"I'm sure it'll be quick," I say to reassure Elva as if I actually know how quickly this can be accomplished. I am in the same position as her, waiting. Whatever, I'm not going to allow this to ruin our trip before it even gets started. She's not the Elva I am used to.

As I walk around the property waiting for a call back from Tina, I think about how lucky she is to have a place like this. I know she uses it as a vacation rental. Why wouldn't she? It really is gorgeous, but so far removed from everything that there is no way someone could live here full time.

Luckily, the phone reception seems decent considering how high up we are in the mountains. I imagine it could get lonely out here. The nearest shop is approximately an hour away. I look down at the drop off on the edge of the mountain where it takes a quick decline on the side of the enormous cabin.

"What do you think it is? About, a 40-foot drop?" says Tom coming up behind me, startling me.

"Perhaps more" I quickly reply.

"No one would survive a drop like that, don't you think?" he questions. What an odd thing to say.

"I guess they probably wouldn't…" I say, eyeing Tom.

I'm saved by a loud ringing from my pocket. It's Tina and I answer while keeping my eye on Tom. "Hi Tina, what did you find out?"

"Hey! Okay, so the code is 2323. Just dial it into the lock enclosure behind the wooden bear on the steps, then pull the latch to open it. The key should pop right out. Call me if you have any problems. Anthony and I are about an hour away. We stopped at the store to grab some wine and goodies for tonight. We got food for a week although I know we won't need it. Can't wait to see you guys!" she says and hangs up.

I make my way over to the wooden bear, avoiding the edge of the mountain and Tom. I follow Tina's instructions and get the key, then unlock the front door.

Tom gathers our bags from the car.

"Finally!" Elva yells and pushes her way into the cabin. She's got to be first.

"This is lovely," I say, openly admiring the decor.

The ceilings are high with wooden beams stretching across the peaks. All the colors are neutral wood tones throughout the cabin. There is an L-shaped leather couch in the middle of the room just a bit to the right of the front door and ahead a large chef's kitchen with a butcher-block island in the center. The cabinets are dark oak. The scene looks like something out of a romance novel.

Double doors lead out to a screened balcony almost triple the size of the kitchen. There is a circular stone fire pit surrounded by cushioned sofas for seating. To the left is a covered hot tub that looks as if it could hold twenty people. I walk to the end of the balcony and look through the screen enclosure. The greenery and silence around us are beautiful, yet somehow unsettling at the same time. There appears to be nothing in the distance. I look down and find a very small stream of water running down the mountain. I wonder if it's fresh water.

I walk back into the cabin to find Elva had already claimed the master bedroom on the main floor.

"You don't mind do you? I mean, I have so much more stuff than you, and Tom and I need the space so…" she trails off.

She knows I packed light since I have only one small bag. Plus, I came alone so I don't really need the master, but it was the way she just assumed I didn't want it bothered me more. "…it's just that we need the larger bed for the two of us. You get it right?" she continued. This time saying it more as if she was asking it was okay.

"Of course. You know I don't need much space. No worries, take it," I say, smiling, but inside I am annoyed with her.

I settle into a smaller room upstairs in the back overlooking where the steep mountain meets the thickness of the woods. Looking out the window, I see the same stream of water I saw from the balcony.

I unpack, hanging up the few articles of clothing I brought in a small closet next to the bed. The bed is a twin with a dark wooden frame with engraved bear claws etched into the upper corners. The right corner of the room houses a mantle with a wood-burning fireplace underneath. I notice ashes from a previous fire are still there. I walk over to a door that leads out to a private balcony with a chair and table just large enough to hold a cup of coffee. Perfect. I can already feel myself unwinding.

"Anyone here?" I hear a woman's voice calling out. "HELLO!?"

It must be Tina. She made better time than she thought since we just spoke a half an hour ago.

I walk downstairs and see her and Anthony walking in, removing their coats and scarves. "Hey! That was fast. Anthony you must have let her drive," I say. Tina's always been known for her lead foot.

"Ha! You bet your sweet behind it was me driving. If I relied on Anthony, who knows where we would have ended up!" she says laughing. Anthony's expression not quite as amused. Tina runs over and gives me a big bear hug. "I missed you!" she says and kisses my cheek.

"Missed you too, girl. It's been a while since we bunked in the same place," I say.

"Hey pretty lady," comes from the master bedroom.

"Elva, wow look at you! You haven't changed not one bit. Look at that forehead. Botox?" Tina says as she rubs her fingers against Elva's forehead genuinely surprised by the lack of stress lines on Elva's face.

"A woman never tells," Elva replies smugly.

"MmHm. Well, I want what your selling!" Tina laughs and winks over at me.

I remember when I introduced Elva to Tina. There was a bit of friendly competition between the two of them. Mostly Elva since she was always competing for some type of attention. But Tina was no push over. Although on the quieter side if you didn't know her well, she knew how to bite back when she needed to. The three of us spent most of our late college years together, with Elva visiting Tina and I at PITT as often as she could.

Elva was easy to like. All of our sorority sisters probably preferred her over Tina and me. She was always invited to events and parties the house threw, but she never actually became a sorority sister. Tina was likeable in that you knew she always had your back. Elva was loyal too, but when it was in her interest. She was self-absorbed and always had an eye out to see who was watching or paying attention to her. A true actress, a showman. Whereas Tina couldn't care less who was watching. She did what she wanted, when she wanted, but within limitations. I looked up to her and respected her for always holding her ground. Together they would make the perfect person - beautiful, brainy, successful, respected, strong. Everything I always thrived to be. Not sure I met all the criteria, but I tried. They made me a better person, and I was glad for it. I knew I could never have Elva's looks, and only half the brains of Tina, but I managed.

I will never forget when the three of us went out to Bootleggers, a bar everyone from PITT hung out in. We were celebrating passing our midterm exams and were looking forward to letting loose. We were hanging out by the pool tables when Tina noticed this super tall and absolutely gorgeous guy across the bar. He was the typical *tall, dark and handsome* kind of guy. He was wearing a long-sleeved polo shirt with the block letters "PITT" written across his chest.

"Tina, look he's from PITT," I said as I nudged her. "He's so cute."
I saw her eyeing him.

Tina became all bent out of shape and embarrassed since Elva and
I were teasing her about not having the guts to go over and talk
to the guy. She wasn't confident enough to just walk over and
spark up a conversation, but we could tell she really wanted to.

"Come on Tina! Put on your big girl panties and just go and talk
to him. He's not going to bite you," Elva said boldly while
continuing to nudge Tina to get her ass moving. She wanted her
to stop stalling.

Tina just couldn't do it. She really didn't date much and when she
did, she was always heart struck. Like a young schoolgirl. Before
Tina and I even got a chance to notice, Elva was already making
her way over to him. She turned her head and winked back at us
while confidently walking toward him. Tina's face said it all – she
was angry. I wasn't sure if it was because she was worried about
what Elva would say to him about her or whether she thought
Elva was planning to hit on the guy for herself.

Unfortunately, Tina's suspicions were correct, Elva was hitting on
him. Tina and I reluctantly watched from across the bar as Elva
whipped her long auburn hair over her shoulders, giggling like a
schoolgirl. She acted like whatever he was saying was the
funniest thing in the world. He never looked in our direction
again. Tina knew then that Elva was not her wing woman, but
rather her competition. Elva was snagging him up for herself.

Tina's face was flushed as if the temperature in the heightened in
the room. Heat was rising from her flustered pink cheeks filled

with anger. She tried to play it off when Elva returned as if it wasn't a big deal, but it was definitely a *big deal.*

"Just another Frat boy I am sure" she said, as if he wasn't worth her time and energy, but I knew better.

Of course, by the end of the night Elva coupled up arm in arm with him.

"She's such a bitch" Tina said, as she watched Elva and Frat boy enter a cab together and leaving the bar and us behind.

We did have some great times together – this just wasn't one of them.

***

"So, what's on the agenda for tonight?" Elva asks Tina as she uncorks a chilled bottle of Sauvignon Blanc from the refrigerator. Then she pours herself a glass and takes a swig of the wine.

"I was thinking we could grill out on the balcony. Anthony, you and Tom could maybe get to know each other a bit over some BBQ preparations, while the ladies have a glass of what Elva is already indulging in and sit on the balcony to catch up." Tina says.

This is exactly what I was hoping for, a low-key trip. "That sounds delightful," I say enthusiastically and grab the bottle from Elva and pour myself a glass. "You witch, you didn't even offer us any! Save some for the others," I tell Elva, half-jokingly.

"Don't worry, there is plenty more where that came from!" Elva says with a wink. She's such a bitch, but I love her. I grab another glass and pour Tina some wine too.

We make our way to the balcony to lounge on the sofas. Elva pulls lights up a cigarette, impressively juggling the lighter and the wine glass in the same hand.

"Aaaah, this is the life ladies" as she says when she exhales her first drag. "No small children running around the house, drinking an adult beverage, and no phone calls from work. I could stay here forever." She finally sounds relaxed.

Tom peaks his head around the corner. "Honey, don't overdo it with the ciggies. You know what the doctor told you," he says with a concerned expression.

"The doctor?" I say concerned.

"Oh, that's enough Tom!" she hollers back. "Isn't he a drag? No pun intended," she says, laughing. "He is so controlling. Don't do this. Can't have this. Wait for this," she says mockingly about Tom. Luckily, he didn't hear her.

Tina and I look at each other confused.

"I thought you two were doing well… What's this all about a doctor?" Tina says.

Elva takes another long drag and puffs out rings above her head. "Don't mind him. He's got a stick up his ass since we left the house. I had a doctor's appointment a month ago. She suggested I take it down a notch on the ciggies, that's all."

Tina and I look at each other again.

"How's Flora?" Tina asks.

"She's beautiful and adorable just like me," Elva says. "But she is very much like Tom…a bit needy."

"Okay, ladies, while the steaks are marinating, I wanted to take this opportunity to toast to a wonderful weekend in the mountains! Grateful and thankful for our gracious host Tina!" Tom says, raising his glass of bourbon and taking a long drink.

I watch as he places the glass down. It's now only half full. Anthony, on the other hand, barely touched his drink.

"What's wrong Anthony, bourbon not to your liking?" I say. Anthony looks at me in disgust. The guys walk back into the cabin.

"What the fuck is up with him?" Elva says as she polishes off her third or fourth glass of wine.

"Nothing. He must be tired. Why do you always have to be so rash, Elva? Your Tom's not a walk in the park either," Tina says in a snippy tone. She gulps her wine.

Great, this is starting off well. "Ladies, come on. We are in one of the most beautiful places with no work stress, let's just let loose and have some fun. No bickering," I say, playing music from my phone.

***

Hours pass and the wind picks up. I look over and Elva is passed out on the sofa, not far from where she started. Tom is having another glass or three of bourbon in the rocker next to her. He seems to always be looking out for her. It doesn't seem controlling as she suggested, more sweet. Tina and Anthony are nowhere to be found. My best guess is they are up in their room.

I glance at my watch and see it's near eleven. I rub my eyes. We arrived hours ago and spent most of the day and into the evening drinking and getting rowdy. I get up without disturbing Elva. Tom gives me a quick wink and head nod acknowledging my departure. I can't tell if he's half asleep or drunk. Who knows? He's still holding a full glass of bourbon in his hand, spilling its contents as he slowly rocks the chair back and forth.

Inside, I see a light shine through the bottom of the door frame, two doors down from mine. I assume it's Tina's room since Elva took the master downstairs. I hear indistinct voices coming from the room as I walk by. It is as if someone is going out of their way to whisper while arguing. It's none of my business. I continue walking and close the door to my room behind me.

I throw myself on what looks like a cushy bed, but, upon landing, discover it's on the firmer side. I don't care. I would have slept on the wooden floor. I am exhausted and a little tipsy. I close my eyes and start to drift off but am abruptly awakened by a long scream. I instantly leap out of the bed and run towards the door, pulling it open and stepping into the dark hallway. I look around but the hall is empty. Even the light from under Tina's bedroom door is now off. Complete silence fills the hallway. Maybe it was in my head, a part of my dream? I go back into my room. My mind wanders. If the scream wasn't part of my dream, what was it? Who could have been screaming? Was Tina in trouble? The scream was definitely from a woman, but the more I push myself to think about it the more the tone of the voice changes in my head. I start to second guess myself. My watch reads 11:25. I put the watch down and turnover in the bed. I must have only been laying down for all of ten to fifteen minutes. How could I have fallen asleep that quickly and already started dreaming?

As I lie in bed and look outside the window at the pale cloudy moon, I begin to feel extremely tired, as if I had been tranquilized. The moon is a perfect circle that slowly, but surely begins to fade, becoming smaller and smaller as my eyes press slowly together. I fall asleep.

CHAPTER FIVE

The morning comes quickly. I wake up to the smell of bacon. My head aches with a hangover. I lurch out of the bed, planting my feet on the floor. It's freezing.

I look outside and can't believe what I'm seeing. It's snowing. I definitely did not prepare for this type of weather. Rifling through my limited wardrobe options, I find my jacket to throw on. I managed to pass out in yesterday's clothes, so I still had my warm wool socks on. I zip up the jacket and open the bedroom door to hear chatter from the downstairs kitchen. Everyone else must already be up.

Tina and Anthony's door is still closed.

"Don't you think it should be a bit darker. I mean look at it." I hear from downstairs.

"You have no idea what you are talking about. Let me handle it!"

As I make my way downstairs, I recall the scream I heard last night. I shake my head to clear the thought but don't succeed. Maybe it was just a dream? No need to relive it or freak out. I am sure it was just a dream, right?

As I get near the bottom of the stairs, I look out over the railing toward the kitchen. Tina is sipping a ridiculously large cup of coffee and sitting in the rocker on the balcony. Tom and Elva are disputing what the correct color is for her coffee.

"In all the years you've been making me coffee, you have no idea how I take it!" Elva yells as she pours more cream into her cup, essentially drinking her cream with a bit of coffee.

"Well good morning sunshine!" Tom says as he sees me approaching. "Someone looks like they slept hard." Elva hits him on the arm.

"She just looks… well rested!" Elva says.

"Hey camper, ready for the hike today?" Tina asks.

"A hi—hike?" I mumble.

"Yes. The first snow just landed overnight, it's the perfect time to go before it freezes over and becomes impossibly slippery," she says.

Good thing I brought my hiking shoes, although I really wasn't planning to use them. It appears my small bag is filled with just the right tricks. It's a bit cold outside for my liking to take a hike, but I guess I have no choice since Tina is already excited about it.

"Sure. I'm going to grab a cup of joe first if you don't mind."

"Oh, naturally, go for it. It doesn't look like Elva is having much more. But if you need cream, that's another story," Tina laughs as Elva hits her arm, knocking half of her coffee out of her gigantic mug.

I pour myself a cup and join the group on the balcony. It's surprisingly warm.

"Oh, don't worry, we have space heaters on out here. It feels like your inside by the fire, doesn't it?" Tina says, watching me peel off my jacket before taking a seat.

"Good idea. This view is phenomenal, it's worth the drive for sure," I say as I take a sip of my piping hot coffee.

"Where is Anthony?" I ask when I'm finally awake enough to realize he isn't among us.

There's a long silence before Tina responds, "He'll be back."

Back from where? I wonder. Her brief response tells me that something is off. Maybe they were arguing last night. Is it possible that something happened between the two of them and he left? Maybe the scream I heard was Tina. Did Anthony leave right after that or this morning? I glance down from the screened enclosure and over to the left to find two parked cars in sight, the silver Jaguar we came in and a green Jeep. I know for sure that the Jeep is Tina's. So where could Anthony have gone without a car in this weather? The mountainside the cabin is set on it far too steep to take a stroll down.

As I look back up, I see Tina staring at me. The look in her eyes seems to be telling me to drop it. Now I am sure something is wrong and that it was her voice I heard from my room. Maybe they were having an argument? Whatever it was, she does not want to talk about it.

"When are we taking this hike?" I ask, changing the subjection.

"If we leave in the next hour or so we'll be right on time to get on the trail and get back before it gets too dark," she says.

"Jesus, how long is this trail? I came to relax, not to work." Elva chimes in. "I have no intention of going hiking anyway, especially in this cold ass weather. You guys are crazy. Have a good time."

"Suit yourself" Tina comments, clearly annoyed. "What about you Cal, you down?"

"Sure, why not? Let's go outside and freeze our asses off. It's not like I've got someone close keeping it warm here!" I reply, laughing at my own stupid joke. Might as well go. What else are we going to do stuck in the house? Plus, it'll give me a chance to catch up with Tina.

"Are you kidding me!?" Elva yells as she drops her cellphone onto the sofa. "No reception! How am I supposed to keep up with work. I can't trust them to work without my direction!" she cries.

It's Saturday, but that does not make a difference to Elva, day or night, rain or shine, week or weekend, she works. So much for taking her focus off work. I look over at Tom who is smirking.

"The snow must have interrupted the cell reception somehow. You are in the mountains after all, shit happens. Maybe you could lay off a bit, relax!" Tina suggests, but then reconsiders. "Maybe try the WIFI."

Elva taps away at her phone. "What's the password? I assume the username is Bear Cabin?" She shoots over a look at Tina.

"It's BearCabin123" says Tina.

"Well, that's not very creative is it, anyone could just hack right in!" Elva's fingers fly across her phone screen. "Nothing!" she yells, "it says that it can't connect. I can't believe this shit!" Elva storms off into the master bedroom, slamming the door behind her.

Tina looks at me and shrugs her shoulders as if to say, "oh well, her loss."

I look over at Tom. He's cleaning up Elva's mess - the wine glasses from the night before and about a dozen cigarette butts with fuchsia lipstick stains. He really is something. I admire the way he cares for her. The way he doesn't allow her moodiness to sway him.

"Get your boots on and let's roll," Tina says as she slams the last of her coffee, then starts pulling on her hiking boots.

"Aren't we going to wait for Anthony?" I say, foolishly. Tina looks at me but says nothing. "Listen, I'm sorry. I shouldn't have brought him up, but it's a bit strange you know, not seeing him the morning after…" I stop.

"After what?" she asks, staring at me.

Why did I bring it up? Why do I always have to be the inquisitive one? She clearly doesn't want to talk about it.

"After what Cal?" she presses.

"Well, I – um, I heard you guys in the room last night — it sounded like maybe you were, um, maybe you were — arguing?" I stammered.

I studied her face before she answered. I couldn't tell if she was annoyed that I was eavesdropping, which I truly wasn't, I was just walking by their room on the way to mine, or whether she was trying to figure out how to deny it. Her long pause told me that she was analyzing what I was going to say next. Like a true engineer she was orchestrating the formula or hypothesis prior to providing her conclusion. I, on the other hand, never had a problem with direct questioning considering my line of work.

"I have no idea what you are talking about Cal," she finally replies.

Really? That's her response? The long dramatic pause for that? A child could have come up with something better.

"Okay, well, I definitely heard something, but I don't want to interfere," I say and leave it at that.

"You don't know what you are talking about so maybe next time mind your business," she says. She won't make eye contact as she pulls on her second hiking boot.

Now I know for sure they were fighting. I am not here to push her buttons or anything, but I know what I heard. Even if I couldn't make out what was said, I know it sounded confrontational. It's not like Tina to react this way or to take this kind of tone with me.

What was the fight about? What was so bad that Anthony left the cabin in the early hours of the morning in freezing weather? It's like he disappeared into thin air. The Jeep is still out front, and I can see his shoes by the front door, although I am sure he brought more than one pair. The entire scenario just doesn't make sense. Why go off on your own? Why not take the car? How is he even familiar enough with the area? Did he and Tina come that frequently? I didn't think so, but the truth was I knew nothing about their relationship.

Tina started dating Anthony about the time her and I stopped texting daily. I barely knew anything about the guy. All Tina told me was that he's Italian, from Brooklyn, and his family has a business in the meat-packing industry. I know what you are thinking and, no, his family does seriously package various types of meats for sale. He is not in the mafia. Apparently, Tina immediately fell for him as soon as she laid eyes on him and his family. She always wanted to have children and a large family, naturally she would gravitate towards someone who valued the same. Plus, it didn't hurt that he was the tall, dark and handsome type that she gravitated towards. They have been together just over a year, and she wants to get married. I don't know whether Anthony feels the same.

Walking back to my room, I pass Tina's. The light is on. I can't be certain the light wasn't already on from earlier, though. I was half asleep. I can see outside the window while I'm putting my boots on. Elva is outside smoking and holding her phone up in different directions. She was probably searching for cell reception. My cellphone falls out of the front pocket of my bag when I stand up. I lean over to pick it up when it lights up. I have a new text message.

"From: Blocked number: I need to talk to you."

That's strange. I try to open the message to reply back asking who they are, but it fails to send. I look at the reception bars on the upper right corner of my phone and confirm there are none. Right. Just like Elva said.

"Are you coming?" Tina yells from downstairs.

I shove the phone in my inner jacket pocket, zip it up, and head downstairs.

"It's a bit nippy out here isn't it?" I say to Tina as I pull out my scarf and wrap it around my neck.

"It's beautiful outside. I wish I could live here year-round," she says happily as if nothing happened earlier.

We walk at a comfortable pace until we are about ten minutes from the front of the cabin to the lower end of the hill.

Tina picks up some speed. "Hustle girl, we need to get down to the bottom then work our way back up towards the top.".

I realize now that this was not going to be the gingerly walk I was hoping for, confirmed by the steepness of the climb, the depth of the woods ahead of us, and Tina's aggressive enthusiasm. "Is there a specific trail we're following?" I hope I sound interested and can distract her from the fact I am already winded.

"This one is about a five- to seven-mile hike. The longer one is on the North end, up the mountain then back down. This one is down then up," she says..

Tina is wearing high-top hiking boots and a pinkish-orange coat. She has thin black gloves on and a black head band holding up her black straight hair tied up in a tight neat ponytail. She looks like she bought the entire outfit right off the mannequin. I, on the other hand, am better suited for sitting or walking, doing mainly low intensity exercises such as walking through a mall. To make matters worse, and more difficult for myself, I am dressed only in a grey jacket with thermal black leggings. Calling them "thermal" is being generous now that I am outside in the snow. I am freezing. I make a mental note to return the leggings as soon as I get back home. In addition, I forgot my gloves, so I'm forced to shove my hands in my pockets to avoid getting hypothermia. *Idiot*.

We are at about the halfway point on the trail, and we haven't spoken much. Tina is slightly ahead of me at an incline like a champion.

"How much longer do we have?" I ask even though I have been tracking the hike on my step counter since we left.

I remember Tina saying we had about seven miles and we are at about three and a half. The incline we are on is about a nine if I was measuring based on treadmills, which I've done all of twice. But it's been a while, so I may be mistaken.

Tina turns towards me to respond, trips over a large rock, and comes tumbling down toward me. I stop and position my legs wide to brace myself. But she knocks me down as well. We roll down the incline for what feels like a few minutes, but I am sure it's only a matter of seconds. I remember rolling down the Pennsylvania hills in the summer when I was a kid. Well, this was the exact opposite. Rather than smooth grass against my back, we are rolling down rocky, graveled terrain. Luckily, we are far enough from the edge of the mountain to avoid that fall. Thank God for that.

"Shit!" I hear Tina right after I hear a *thud* that is clearly her tumble being stopped by a large stump in front of her. It stopped my roll too and I landed directly on top of her.

"Fucking hell!" she grunts and pushes me off her.

We lie on the ground side by side, perfectly still now, breathing heavily. It crosses my mind that I will now need to make up for the loss of progress on the trail. I look above us and see tall trees capped with snow. It's quite beautiful from this angle. I never would have chosen quite this view, but here I am and it's not so bad. Better than walking that damn incline.

The sun is just about at its highest point, which tells me we have been at this was about two hours or so. Seems like it should have taken less time, but, considering the incline, it was about right. I look over at Tina who is just lying there looking up towards the sky as well. She's tense. Maybe she's hurt. Or maybe she's mad at me for distracting her by talking while on that incline. But I sensed more to her than that. I look again and see tears rolling down her face.

"He's leaving me" she says flatly.

And there it is.

CHAPTER SIX

Tina sits up and is now sobbing. I don't know whether to hug her or just allow her to just sit there and cry it all out. I sit up and put my hand on her knee. We sit there for a good few minute in silence as she weeps. It all makes sense now. Why she has been so tense and snippy with me. I know Elva annoys her, but she never gets annoyed with me. The closed-door whisperings, the mystery behind Anthony leaving, and that scream. I am certain it was them fighting and she was likely too embarrassed to admit it. Surely, she knew I wouldn't judge her, but she probably didn't want Elva to catch wind of it as she wouldn't easily let it go. Instead, she would push and pry until Tina cracked. It was Elva that enjoyed the drama, not Tina.

I look around, absorbing the thickness of the trees around us. We had more miles on the trail back toward the cabin than I had initially thought or hoped. Not just because we both plummeted backwards enough to add additional time. There was really nothing in sight to measure our distance besides my step counter. It confirmed we had some ways to go if we wanted to make it back before it started to get dark. I realize that going back the same way we came would be more challenging, so we proceeded forward.

"Are you alright?" I finally ask when I can't bear the silence any longer and I see she has stopped sobbing.

"I'm not" she said flatly. "He's leaving me. I—I can't--- I can't give him what he wants." She starts to tear up again.

"What is it he wants?"

"Children!" she screams and jumps up, dusting the dirt off her clothes and angrily kicking into the ground.

I really don't know what to say. I had no idea what the circumstances were between them, but I can only guess that they have been trying with no such luck or are having fertility issues.

"Did you—does he—are you both, were you trying?" I ask, stupidly.

"Yes, well sort of. I had, I was—pregnant, but I had a," she starts, "…a miscarriage."

"When we went to see my OBGYN, she confirmed that I have an issue which hinders my ability to get or stay pregnant…" she cries, "I am infertile, Cal."

"Oh, Tina, I am so very sorry, I had no idea, I—" say as she cuts me off.

"Well, how could you have known, you…" she says, stopping mid-sentence.

"I, what?".

"Nothing."

"I, what? Tell me what you are trying to say. Stop dancing around your words." I say, annoyed with her.

"You were never around, Cal! When I called you to talk, you were always too busy, so how could you have known when I didn't even have the chance to tell you?" she shouts.

Wow, how did I end up being the bad guy here? I need to tread lightly with her. She is clearly at a breaking point. I know if I say anything else in defense I would be in the wrong, even if it may be called for.

"I'm sorry. I should have been there for you," is what I finally say.

It's the truth. I didn't mean to disconnect from her, but I became totally disconnected from everyone. All I did during COVID was work since the world was on a lockdown. Work became everything. When the time came to get back to the real world, I didn't have to and chose not to. I continued to work from home and used work as my excuse for why I was too busy to meet up with friends and family.

Tina and Elva both live hours from me so I knew they couldn't just stop by randomly for a quick visit. Seeing them meant going out of my way to schedule a time to hang out, which I'd avoided for some reason. As a result, we never saw each other until now. Elva said it's been a year, but she's wrong, it's been longer. I saw her briefly about a little over a year ago when she visited her grandmother and stopped by the house with Flora. Other than that, it's been over two years. Now is my opportunity to be the friend I used to be to Tina, the friend I still want to be.

"Are you okay?" I ask again.

"I'll be fine" she replies, but she really doesn't seem fine. "He wants a family and that is not something I can physically give to him, so he is leaving me."

How fucking selfish of him. How does he know it's not his fault she can't have kids? Maybe his sperm isn't strong enough rather than it being her eggs. I feel myself getting a bit defensive on Tina's behalf.

"Why can't you adopt?"

"ADOPT?!" she yells, "Yeah right, Cal, you really think an Italian man with a large family is okay with *adoption*?" she adds. She may have a point. "The last thing on his mind would be to adopt and his mother would NEVER go for adoption, especially since he is the eldest son. He needs to keep the family name going, to produce with his own fucking seed!" she screams, a bit hysterically. "We were going to get married, nothing fancy, just quickly at the courthouse before the baby came, but…" she says, stopping mid-sentence.

Damn! This is deeper than I thought. You got his mother in the picture now. She may bite my head off if I open my mouth about it again. "I see."

"So that's it, he's gone." She turns and starts to climb up toward the mountain.

We walk side by side in silence. At this point, I think we both prefer it. We come to a sign pointing right. The sign reads "Medical Emergency." We continue walking passed the sign. I look to the right but don't see any signs of structure or something that may provide assistance for a medical emergency. We carry on about another few miles and I am starting to limp in my right leg. Tina seems to be walking straight without a missing a step.

I calculate how far we've walked and we should be at the cabin by now. I look at Tina and she suddenly seems disoriented. We stop.

"Do you think we passed our turn?" I ask her.

Tina is pale and doesn't reply.

"Tina, are you okay?"

She slides down next to me. Still not speaking. Shit. I didn't bring any water with me. Unfortunately, sundown is approaching, and I need to get us off this trail before it gets too late.

"Tina, do you think you can lift yourself up enough so I can carry you? We can walk back to where we saw that medical emergency sign." I say, though I'm unsure if she actually can. I pull my phone out of my pocket and try to find a signal. No bars. How did we have such good reception yesterday?

Tina is semi-responsive as I kneel back down to hold her head up. "Hey bud, are you with me?" I say. There is no way I can physically walk this incline and carry her at the same time. This isn't a good place to be stuck on an unfamiliar trail in what feels like the middle of nowhere.

It starts to feel colder as the sun progresses downward. Soon we won't have any sunlight to help guide us back to the cabin.

Tina's eyes blink open and she seems to be gaining some strength back. She sits up gingerly.

"Hey! There you are! You had a bit of a slip. You think you can lift yourself up?" I ask, hopeful.

"What am I doing on the ground again?" she asks confused.

"Seems we spent a bit more time lying on the ground than walking today," I reply with a chuckle, happy to be in better spirits and optimistic we aren't actually going to be stuck out here all night.

She cautiously lifts herself off the ground, planting both hands flat on the ground behind her as she shifts her body weight to the right of herself and pushes her arms upward. I stand next to her, grabbing her right arm to help steady her.

"There you go, easy does it," I say.

I take her right arm and wrap it around my neck to ease some of the stress off her feet and begin to walk up the mountain slowly, watching for rocks, snow, or anything that could toss us both back to the ground.

We soon reach the point where turning right would place us on the road to her cabin. Tina must know the way as she curves towards that direction. I wasn't sure we would make it prior to losing daylight, but I'm glad we did. I smell something sweet, yet tangy—something very familiar. I look up to see Anthony leaning against Tina's Jeep, smoking a blunt. There he is boyfriend of the year. Where the hell has he been?

"Ladies, there you are!" he says as he takes another deep drag of the rolled up blunt. Prick. That's the best he could come up with? How about a little help, I'm only here dragging your girlfriend, ex-girlfriend, whatever, back to the cabin while you smoke a joint without a care in the world. He could clearly see that Tina was hurt, but he doesn't bat an eye. His arrogance amazes me as he, in sloth-like motion, flicks the butt of his joint to the ground somewhere into the deep woods and looks at us. *"Only you can prevent forest fires,"* said Smoky the Bear, I remember we were brainwashed this in elementary school, but it's clear that he didn't care about it.

"A little help over here!" I say angrily, pissed that I even have to insist that help is needed.

He walks over and lazily retrieves Tina's right arm from my neck and swings it over his shoulders. She's awake and conscious but still weak. I can tell she is relying heavily on Anthony to get back to the cabin. I grip her left arm to make sure she is stable while walking.

I push open the door to find Elva sitting on the sofa with a glass of red wine watching TV on the 85" flat screen in front of her.

She jumps up when she sees the condition Tina arrives in and sprints over.

"Oh My God! What the hell happened to her?" she asks.

"We had a little bit of a tumble," I say, looking at Tina as she eyeballs me with a look of *"please don't tell her another word."*

Anthony and I settle Tina on the sofa, pushing a pillow under her lower back for support and another one under her head.

"She's going to be okay…grab her some water, will you?" I ask Elva.

"I knew it wasn't a good idea to go out there. Look at the thickness of the snow now, you guys are insane. So much for a workout!" she says. "That's why it's best to just stay here and relax, maybe a glass of wine would be helpful?"

"Elva!" I yell, "just grab her a water, please. We didn't ask for your humble opinion." Night brings with it more snow. A brush of sadness comes over me while I finish up in a warm shower. I step out and retrieve a plush white towel from the rack. I take a moment to appreciate that there are towel warmers installed. Everything else about this place suddenly feels so cold.

I think how things have changed between all of us. We are all so distant from each other now. We used to be easy-going together, constantly laughing, enjoying each other's company. Now it feels strained, forced at times. Tina and Elva are on edge for reasons I cannot fully comprehend. I don't know the men well enough to judge if their behavior is typical for them or not.

A scream and a loud smash break through my thoughts. I run into the bedroom and throw my housecoat on, wrapping it tightly around my waist. It's freezing. The floorboards sting on my bare feet as I run out into the hallway.

"What's going on?" I yell out in fear, although I don't see anyone in the hallway outside of my room.

I run down the stairs to where I left the group a little over an hour ago to rest a bit and shower. I see everyone standing except Tina. I push my soaking wet hair off of my shoulders and tighten my housecoat around my waist. Elva is cupping her mouth with her left hand and holding the sofa with her right as if she might collapse forward. I take another step closer. Drip. Drip. Drip. The water slips off my skin onto the wood flooring. Anthony is kneeling with his head face-down against the sofa. It sounded as if he was sobbing softly, but I couldn't see his face to confirm there were tears.

My heart starts pounding as if it would leap out of my chest. I take another step forward, and another. I look down and see Tina, lying motionless on the sofa, deeply embedded into its cushions. What is going on? Why is Anthony crying? What is happening? Tina's face is expressionless and paler than the snow hitting against the windowpane. Gasping, I raise my right hand to touch her. She feels cold. Her lips appear to be turning a light bluish hue.

"Is she dead?" Elva cries out in panic.

I look up blankly staring at Elva's horrified face. I look towards Anthony.

"Well?" Elva screams at me as if I am the most capable of handling the situation despite none of us having a medical degree.

I take a step back and something electric, eager, deep down inside comes over me as I yell "Call 911, we need an ambulance *NOW!*" Why the hell has no one done so already? How long have they been down here with her knowing she was unconscious? I turn in circles looking for my phone, forgetting where I left it initially, then remembering it was in my inner jacket pocket. I run to the door and retrieve the phone. I start to dial 911, putting the phone on speaker. The dial tone is flat. No reception.

"*SHIT!*" I yell. "Elva, Anthony, check your phones to see if you have a signal. My phone is useless! We need to get medical help, *immediately!*" I scream over to them in a panic.

Tom is nowhere in sight.

I can't believe this is happening. I can't wrap my head around what exactly *is* happening and what *has* happened. I just spoke to her before heading upstairs to shower. She was lying on the sofa, clearly in pain from our hobble back over to the cabin, but she was wide awake, talking, even joking about how dumb it was the way she fell. She drank a full glass of water right before laying her head back down on the sofa. She looked okay, just a bit tired. Sure, her knee had a nice black and blue mark on it, some scrapes here and there and a bit of swelling, but nothing major. Nothing life threatening. We could have tumbled down the side of the mountain, falling to our death, but we managed to avoid it. How did she become so ill to have… Surely this is all a sick joke.

Elva and Anthony are both searching for a signal on their cellphones. Anthony runs out of the cabin, leaving the door open behind him allowing the cold air to enter along with a gust of wind carrying flakes of snow.

"I—I have nothing, no signal. It's d- dead," Elva stammers. Then she runs outside to see if Anthony has any better luck with his reception.

Anthony is pacing back and forth in front and around the cabin holding his cellphone up, over and around himself to gain any type of signal. He shakes his head.

"That's it! I'm getting her in the car and driving out of here to the first hospital!" Elva yells as she grabs her purse from the side table and motions Anthony to come back into the cabin to help her with Tina's lifeless body.

"Wait!" I yell, "We have no idea where the closest hospital is. You'll be driving in circles down the mountain just looking for it, if you can even get down with all the snow and ice in your Jag. "Here." I take the keys off the kitchen counter and throw them to Elva. "Use the Jeep, it's has a 4x4. if we have a chance of getting through the snow or over ice without sliding, it's definitely better," I say hopefully reassuring myself. "There's was a sign—um—I saw it during our hike, for emergencies. I don't know where it leads, whether it's a building or what, but it was about, um—2 to 3 miles up the mountain on the trail, not sure how to get there by car…" I say.

Anthony reenters the cabin, slipping on the ice at the foot of the front door.

"I'll go with you two," I say.

"Absolutely not," says Anthony. "Someone needs to stay here in case reception comes back to call for help. If we all go together and something happens, no one will ever know we were here."

He lifts Tina off the sofa and carries her to the Jeep. He's right, but how can I just sit and wait for their return… if they return in this hellish weather. There's half a foot of snow and plenty of ice on top of what was there this morning. I start to doubt that not even the Jeep can successfully get through. But what other choice do we have? We can't just sit here with her lifeless body and wait -

for what? For all of us to freeze? For her to actually *die*? I shake my head. If we get help now, maybe she will be okay. I watch as the headlights from the Jeep vanish into the night as Anthony and Elva drive off to seek help. I pinch myself to make sure I am not in a nightmare.

CHAPTER SEVEN

It's half-past six as I anxiously glance down at my phone. Still no signal. I pace back and forth trying to wrap my head around what *is* happening. It just does not add up. I was hiking with Tina. We fell and rolled down the hill. When we realized we were okay, she got up and continued walking. Then she collapsed. I replayed the scenario over and over in my head. Somehow, we made it back to the cabin. She then laid down. She seemed tired and bruised but okay. I must have missed something important. Later, I came downstairs and saw her lying on the sofa, lifeless. Was she unconscious or dead? We didn't try to find a pulse or check if she was breathing. *Idiots.*

Did she hit her head on the way down during the tumble? I remember watching her roll before she ran into me, and then we both rolled downhill. I can't recall her hitting her head against anything. She never even complained about her head hurting or anything like that, so maybe it wasn't *that* fall. Maybe it was the second fall when she fainted. Again, I can't remember whether Tina hit her head on anything. Wait, I caught her before she went all the way down. She couldn't have hit her head then, right? So, what else could it have been? Could someone literally die of a broken heart? That seems like nonsense, but in this case, she was awfully emotional, upset from stirring up the past with Anthony, talking about the miscarriage and his recent threat to leave her. I stop suddenly remembering the scream I heard the night prior. It literally scared me out of my bed. I thought about the argument I heard coming from Tina and Anthony's room earlier. Could something that happened there have triggered this? Did he hit her? I shake my head in disbelief. Surely, she would have mentioned him hitting her—or would she have? She's been mysterious lately, closed off, unlike herself.

I wish I knew more about Anthony. Tina never mentioned that he was violent but, apparently, she didn't mention lots of things. Maybe he hurt her, caused her to bleed internally… maybe he hit her hard enough that it made her lose her balance during our walk, enough to trip and fall the way that she did. She seemed off the entire time. Oddly, when we left, Anthony was nowhere in sight. Where did he go and why did Tina not want to talk about it? Maybe when we saw Anthony back at the cabin he was remorseful after their argument, but then why would he have barely helped me get her back into the cabin?

***

As I continue to pace through the cabin, I make sure to lock all the doors and windows as I pass them. The snow is still coming down aggressively. The interior of the cabin is now almost as cold as the outside and there aren't any more logs to toss into the fireplace and the gas is not turning on from the burner.

A *creak* makes me jump.

Creeeeeakkk!

It sounds like someone or something is walking around upstairs. I creep up the stairs, holding on to the staircase's railing with my right hand and my phone in my left, as if I planned to attack someone with the phone should they jump out at me. The floorboards upstairs are uneven. I remember tripping over a lifted board right after the final step from the top of the stairs. I hear it again.

There's dead silence. The creaking stops. I stop walking and turn my head to look over my shoulder but see nothing. *Thank goodness.*

I stopped directly in front of Tina and Anthony's room. The door is shut but the light is on. I place my right hand slowly on the door handle and lightly turn it. There is a hesitation as if someone is holding the other end of the knob. I push forward. I enter the room. I am alone.

I look around to find a small reading light on the desk is on. There is a double bed next to a window, the desk immediately to the right of the bed, and a small three-piece bathroom. There isn't much in the room besides a small duffle bag in the closet and a purse on the bed. I gravitate to the small black purse on the bed. Some of its contents are already poured out in an unorganized fashion. I sit on the bed, placing the crossbody bag on my lap and begin to search inside it. I pull out a matching black wallet, hand sanitizer, four lip glosses, a small digital organizer and a cellphone. I know it is Tina's phone.

I turn on the phone, confirming there is still no reception. I hear a *BING* and feel a vibration at makes me jump as a message comes through. It scared the hell out of me. How could she have received a message? Maybe it was an older message she hadn't yet checked that just came through when I started up the phone? We were gone for most of the morning, it's possible Tina never checked her phone.

A chilling thought crosses my mind—what if the message is from the person that may have hurt her or killed her? I take a deep breath, and I blow the air out of my mouth slowly to calm my nerves. I click on the message.

Blocked number: I have no idea why I haven't heard from you… I really need to talk to you. It is very important. You don't need to do this Tina.

I put down the phone and take another deep breath, but this time hold it in for a few seconds before releasing it.

*You don't need to do this Tina…*What the fuck is going on here? I reread the message again. Who sent this message and why is the caller blocked? What could be so important? Why not just call her instead? I see no missed calls on her phone. And, if the message was urgent, why send it from a blocked number unless you were hiding something? Questions fill my head. Suddenly, I remember a message I received earlier. I scroll to the top of my text messages to find the last one I received before I lost reception.

From: Blocked number. I need to talk to you.

I go into the details option in my phone's settings but forgot that the details aren't available without a cell signal. If I could just get some reception back on my phone I could see when the messages were sent, but right now there is no way to tell. I try to pull up the same details from Tina's iPhone, but the problem is the same. No reception.

What could this be about? Could it really be a coincidence that someone had texted both Tina and I around the same time with very similar messages? I saw my message right before we left for the hike, but I couldn't send a message back or access any of the text details to do so. Perhaps, Tina got hers at the same time. She wouldn't have known since she didn't have her phone with her all day and the message was marked unread right before I viewed it. She must have kept her phone in the room the entire time. Although the message felt like it just came through. I can't be certain.

"Hello?" I hear a voice downstairs.

I shove Tina's phone and the other contents back into her purse and try to reposition it and its contents on the bed back the way I found them. Not that she would notice, but if Anthony made his way back up to the room, I wouldn't want him to know I was snooping. I slid out of the room slowly closing the door behind me. *Creeeaaakkkk....* The sound comes from the place my foot landed as I exited the room. *Shit!*

"Hello all, where are you guys??" a male voice says.

I turn and look over the stair railing.

"Tom?" I say, slightly relieved to no longer be alone in this dark, cold cabin. Though, I could have used a few more minutes to finish looking through Tina's room for potential clues or something to help explain this incident.

"Yeah, what's going on?" He shakes the snow from his coat and off his boots. "Where is everyone?" he asks as I make my way down the stairs, still in my housecoat, hair less wet but slightly crispy in places.

"What's going on? Where are the others?" he asks again with more concern.

He looks run down. It hadn't even crossed my myself to ask where he was when the others were still downstairs in the cabin. The entire day felt like a blur.

"Hi—I—um, where have you been?" I ask.

"What do you mean where have I been, where the hell have you guys been? You left earlier in the morning on a hike that should have taken no more than two to three hours," he says. "I went out to find you two idiots. The wind and snow started to pick up and I was concerned."

Interesting… It's been hours since we left and hours since we returned and somehow Tom is just now getting back to the cabin. He would have frozen to death by now had he been outside the entire time on foot looking for us. It's so cold. And did he take the same trail we did? My guesstimate of our time on the trail and after isn't solid but it felt off. He may have gone to search for us when he realized we were gone longer than we should have been. I wanted him to explain, but first I needed to tell him what happened to Tina.

"Tom…" I start, "…something happened—to Tina—she's not okay. She—I don't know if she's going to make it." I watch his expression drop, but then his frown turns to more of a smirk.

"What the hell are you talking about? Is this another stupid prank?"

I wish this was a prank, but it is not. We used to play tricks on each other back in the day when things were a bit lighter than they are now.

"Where is everyone?" he asks again, more impatiently.

I sit Tom down and explain exactly what happened, from the moment Tina and I left the house on the hike this morning, to finding her lifeless body on the sofa. I left out the part about her fight with Anthony and the miscarriage as it really was none of his business. Tom looks at me in complete disbelief, slowly gets up, and walks to the kitchen. He removes two crystal glasses from the cabinet and pours both of us a glass of bourbon. He hands me one and downs his. He wipes off his mouth, just standing there as if waiting for the punch line.

"Then Anthony and Elva left with Tina, taking her to the emergency center or something," I say. "You must have seen it during your walk back…" I add as I watch Tom's expression just as I finish. Surely, he would have seen the sign since it was close to the cabin.

"I—I may have recalled seeing a sign," he says blankly. He *may* have recalled the sign? Is he serious, how could he have missed it? If he was on the same trail that we were both on, which was really the only trail in sight, easily accessible, he *must* have seen the sign. There was nothing else out there like it. It was the only sign we saw. He *must* have seen it – unless he was on another trail.

"So, you didn't see the sign?"

"Damn it, Cal, I do not remember what I saw. I was just looking for you gals. You could have fallen off the cliff for all I would have known!" he yells.

I'm not sure what to believe.

"How were you gone for so long, di—did you go somewhere else first?" I ask, watching Tom's expression go from a frown to full force anger.

"What the hell is this Cal—some type of an interrogation? I am not your enemy here! You're not in a courtroom, so fucking cool it! What do you think I killed her or something?" he asks, angrily, then starts to laugh hysterically.

I get off the sofa, taking a step away from Tom. What kind of comment is that? Could he have killed Tina somehow? Could he have hidden somewhere outside or lied in waiting for us to return so he could murder her while the others weren't looking? I hadn't seen Tom since we left for the hike, he could have been anywhere, at any point. What would be his motive? Did he hear Anthony and Tina arguing through the door and saw or heard something I missed, something that triggered him? Was he helping Anthony get away, making it an easier break from Tina? The pieces of the puzzle aren't falling together for Tom to be a killer. I can't think of a proper motive.

Tom watches my uneasy movements through the cabin. "Listen, *very* bad choice of words okay. I'm no murderer!" he says, holding both hands up as if to show me they're clean. "I simply tried to help as Elva was very concerned about you two, so I went to go find you that's it. I'm not in the best of shape, so the walk up hill wasn't easy on me, or my knees... I took a break, continued, then eventually came back here. That's it, okay?" he says defensively.

Truth be told, I really did not think it could be Tom. He was a bit pathetic and needy, but not a killer. Not sure he truly had a bad bone in his body. He followed Elva around like a puppy dog. If she said "sit" he would sit. If she said "lay down" his back would be flat on the ground, legs up. If she wanted him to hike through the snowed trail looking for her girlfriends, off he went. So, it was highly likely he was actually out there looking for us. His bum knee did not make it easier. I remember he broke it in a ski accident a few years back when he ate shit on the final steep slope.

I nod and let the subject drop. Snow piles deeper around the cabin as the night goes on. I dry my hair and put fresh joggers and my thickest wool sweater to keep warm.

Tom is still in the kitchen, sitting on the bar stool, drinking what may be his sixth bourbon when I return. I sit beside him and push a glass over toward him. He pours me a drink. I sit there sipping and thinking. How could this have happened? Why did this happen? Where are the others now and where were they all when they weren't in my sight earlier? Who sent those text messages? Why did they send them? Were they meant to be a warning? Was someone trying to give Tina a heads up on what was coming her way? Maybe to try and warn her that she was going to *die*?

CHAPTER EIGHT

As I lift myself off the bar stool, the clock on the wall strikes 11:45 pm. Tom had passed out on the sofa drunk as a skunk. I look again over at the clock. The others should have been back already, right? I'm anxious and fearful. The roads are likely in no condition to drive on, what if they got in an accident or got stuck? Maybe they couldn't find the emergency help center so they drove further out. Maybe the car went off the cliff and no one heard it. As the old riddle goes, when a tree falls in the forest does it make a sound? The likely answer is yes, how could it not? But if no one is around to hear it, what good does it do anyway? I bite my nails. Blood leaks from under my fingernail. I'm angry that Tom and I are just sitting here waiting—well, mainly me since Tom had passed out on the couch. But what am I waiting for?

I put my hand back up towards my mouth but stop myself. My eyes open wide and my heart races as I get the urge to go and look for them. What if they need help? I would be the only person that knows where they were heading. I hurry over to Tom and nudge him, hoping to wake him up.

He grunts and turns away to face the back of the sofa. I leave him to search for Elva's car keys on the side table where I thought I saw her drop them earlier but no luck. I look in the kitchen and open the balcony door. That was a mistake. I tremble and immediately slam the door shut after a quick peek outside at the patio table. I walk into the master bedroom to see if Elva left her purse. Nothing. Maybe she took the keys with her in her purse when she left with Anthony and Tina. But why would she leave me stranded here without a car? Well, they were panicked and in a hurry, so anything is possible.

Tom is actively snoring now. I'm surprised slamming the patio door did not wake him. Maybe he has a set of keys. I start tapping his shoulder to wake him up. He doesn't so much as twitch. I move my hand down lightly over the exterior of his pockets, to feel whether keys are there. Still nothing. I resort to rolling him over on his side to check his front pockets. As my hand is down in a pocket, Tom's hand cups mine as if to bring my hand over to his groin.

"Ohhh, Elva, baby…" he says in his sleep.

"Eww" I squeal, yanking my hand from his pocket and far away from his groin. *Where the fuck are the damn keys?*

I check Tom's jacket's pocket but find nothing. I slide on my boots and throw my jacket over my sweater and head outside. I make my way over to the driver's side of the Jag while wiping the window to try and remove the snow. I look inside the car and see the keys in the ignition. What the hell? I pull on the door handle. It sticks but comes open. I jump into the driver's seat and immediately shut the car door. For a moment, I just sit rub my hands together, huffing into them. It must be at least -5 F outside at this point and without gloves frost bite it a serious possibility. Once I can feel my hands again, I try to start the ignition.

It rumbles as the engine tries to turn over. I try again. More rumbling, then silence. It's dead. I'm not surprised. It's covered in snow. Even if it started, I am not sure I would find a way to dig it out.

"Fuck!" I yell as I hit the steering wheel with both hands.

This is not how this trip was supposed to go, it was supposed to unite us! Tina, poor Tina, thoughtful, beautiful inside and out. What the fuck happened to her?! I hit the steering wheel again as if it would somehow turn the car on magically. I kick my feet out against the brake in frustration. A small bottle rolls out from under the seat and hits my foot. I bend over to pick it up. It's a prescription bottle - brownish orange, white cap, white label.

Patient: Elva Bronson, take two tablets once nightly 3 hours prior to going to bed" I turn the bottle and see it's from a pharmacy in New York. I continue to rotate the bottle, Zolpidem, side effects may occur. I put the bottle down in the cupholder. Zolpidem. I try to place where I knew it from. I pick the bottle back up. May cause drowsiness. Do not operate heavy machinery Refills: 2. What is this stuff? Is this a sleep aid of some sort? But why keep it in the car and since when does Elva take sleeping aids? Poor girl. I know Tom has been trying to get her to take a step back from work, but sleeping pills…? *Ugh.*

I look in the back seat and around the interior of the car for anything else that may help me but find nothing. Then I get out of the car, taking the keys with me. I hurry back inside the cabin and lock the door. As I remove my jacket and boots, I turn to find Tom no longer on the sofa. I take a quick spin around he is somewhere else in sight but I'm alone. Where could he have gone? He was completely knocked out when I last him a few minutes ago.

Maybe he woke up and stumbled to the bathroom or something. I peek into the master, cautiously in case he was nude or showering or whatever. But I find no sight of Tom. He couldn't have left. I would have seen him leave. The Jag was directly facing the front door of the cabin… unless he went out the back and into the woods. It's so dark though. It wouldn't be possible to see unless you had a flashlight. He was really in no condition to go walking outside, especially with that 40-foot drop on one side of the cabin. A chill passes through me at the thought of the plummet. This cozy cabin is starting to feel more like the little house of horrors.

I look at the table next to the sofa to see if Tom left anything behind. It dawns on me that his phone has a flashlight and didn't need a signal, just battery power. God, he would have needed more than that to guide his way, perhaps a longer nap and an Advil.

But why leave? Was he tired of waiting? Worried about Elva and left to go find her? How could he have been able to in his condition, a severe drunken state, unless…*unless he faked it*. What if he wasn't drunk at all? Here I go again, down the rabbit hole of my own crazy thoughts. I force myself to think clearly. I saw him drinking bourbon like a fish. He seemed convincingly drunk. I didn't count the glasses, but I assumed from the contents left in the bottle he drank six or so glasses on his own. That was certainly enough to get someone drunk, even a seasoned drinker. Maybe he only wanted me to think he was drinking more but really pouring them out and pretended to pass out so I would get comfortable and give him an opportunity to kill me like he did Tina.

The loud creaking sound from before is back. But this time it's louder, closer. I grab a kitchen knife from a block on the counter. More creaking, this time directly overhead. Was it Tom? Is he going to attack me? Is his plan to just kill everyone, one by one? Who would be next, Anthony or Elva? He wouldn't dare hurt his precious Elva.

I slowly make my way up the stairs while gripping the knife. I am the stupid girl in the horror movie that hears an intruder and walks right toward the killer, right into his trap only to die from the knife she brings to defend herself.

The creaking gets louder but now it sounds like it's behind me. I turn to look but a hand covers my mouth, and something covers my eyes. I can't breathe. I can't scream. I gasp for air thinking I may hyperventilate or suffocate right. My nose is covered too. I drop the knife and go limp as I'm dragged into a room.

"Shhhh" a voice says. "Don't scream or…"

Or what you'll kill me like you did Tina?

"I'm going to uncover your mouth go. Do not scream." the voice repeats.

Just as I take a breath I hear, "Cal-bear, shh." I'm pushed up against what feels like a man's chest. A muscular one. My breath starts to echo his. Each inhale and exhale come together as one.

"Do not scream."

The panic starts to fade. We sit silently for what feels like hours, but it could only be a few seconds. He is breathing onto my neck.

Stretching my leg out, I kick what appears to be a wall directly in front of me but make no noise. His warm breath moves along my jaw to my lips. I feel something rise up inside of me. The voice sounds so familiar.

"Joe, is that you?" I say softly.

"Shhh, quiet Cal-bear. You're going to be okay."

CHAPTER NINE

"This is Joe." Tina nudged me as she pointed at him. "He's my loser big bro," she said laughingly as she poked him in the side. I thought about how nice it was to have someone to poke fun with like that. That must come with having a sibling who was at least somewhat close in age.

"Hey. I… I am Calista, but my friends call me Cal," I said finally as I smiled and timidly put out my hand.

He didn't seem to notice my nerves. I could literally see all of his pearly white teeth when he smiled.

"Cal, hey, nice to meet you. I am *THE* big brother, Joe Williams. I'm sure Tina has told you all about me," he said smugly, but in an oddly endearing way. She never mentioned him once, but there was no reason to point that out. Tina gave me a pointed look.

"Um, yeah, sure she did…" I replied as I rubbed my side where Tina's boney elbow dug into me.

"Do you drink?" he asked me.

I didn't drink much. I never had more than the table wine at my parents' house growing up. They frowned on it. Likely because my Uncle Mike was a borderline alcoholic. My father was always worried about bringing the stuff into the house, especially when he was around. He stayed with us for well over a year, so my father got used to locking the stuff up and eventually taking it out of the house completely. It didn't matter to me, drinking or not, but I tended to avoid it.

"Oh yeah, sure I do," I said, shrugging. Not sure why I felt like I needed to lie.

"So, what should I get you ladies? Let's see, we have our finest available - Bush Light or Pabst Blue Ribbon. They are the champagne of beers don't you know?" he said, laughing as he popped the top of one open and downed it like it was water.

"Um, I- I'll have the one you are having…," I said.

Joe handed over two aluminum cans of beer our way. It really was nothing like champagne. In fact, it was disgusting, but I drank it anyway. Nothing like a little bit of peer pressure to help push the stuff down. Champagne my ass. PITT restricted the use of alcohol in the residence halls to those who were 21 years old or older. Must have been the best we could get with the restrictions.

As the night went on, I found myself chugging the beer upside down after losing a bet to Joe. Not sure how I got to that point, but I remember Joe and Tina cheering me on. I was oddly proud of myself for not vomiting. My parents would be so proud.

By the end of the night, Joe, Tina, and I found ourselves sitting on a dingy sofa pulled out onto the front lawn of one of the fraternity houses. We spent the night talking, laughing, playing drinking games, and just having a good time together. I watched in amazement as Joe balanced a red solo cup on his forehead while it was filled with some concoction while hopping around on one leg. Apparently, the point was for one of his fraternity brothers to land a white plastic ball into the cup while he did so. I had to admit, it was impressive. Those were the days, carelessly easy and fun. No obligations, just good times. I don't think I ever saw Joe without a smile on his face and I don't think I ever saw Tina laugh harder than she did at him.

***

We have only been this close once before. It was after the Pike's Frat threw their season opener and Joe was visiting for the event from Florida. He was there helping his fraternity brothers host the event. A type of recruitment, but Joe was really only there for a good time. He hated Florida's humidity during the summer months and would have made any excuse to leave. He always found an excuse to make his way north. With Tina being here in school and his brothers in the frat, it was easy.

I never really wanted a boyfriend. I had a few in the past, but never felt anything more for them than friendship. Not sure why, I guess I just couldn't force it. When I first met Joe, I felt like I had known him my entire life. If it was what love at first sight was like I definitely felt something more than I wanted to admit. However, because of my friendship with Tina, I never did or said anything about my potential feelings for Joe since he was her big brother and the last thing she would want to hear from another girl is how cute he was.

But one night, after a party and too many beers, Tina, Joe, and I stayed behind to hang out. There was a swing set in the Pike's yard along with a large couch. That couch was not made for the outdoors and was pretty hideous. I sat on the swing and held on to its chains, kicking my feet and pushing myself forward. I felt like a kid again. Tina had passed out on the couch. Under different circumstances, Tina would not have been caught dead laying on a couch like that since she was a germaphobe. I wasn't going to leave her there, but I was not quite ready to leave yet.

"Tina?" I shouted from the swing, "Come swing with meeee!" yelling at the top of my lungs in a clearly tipsy state of mind.

"Leave her to it, they basically give DUIs for walking drunk through this campus nowadays," Joe says, sounding amused.

He grabbed my waist and pushed me. My feet swung up and I leaned back into the swing as it took me higher. Joe ran to the front of me and grabbed at my feet while I was swinging forward. I laughed and kicked at him. I decided to jump off the swing, thinking he would move out of the way. He stood in place, and I toppled onto him, knocking us both to the ground. We laid there laughing until I finally rolled off him and to the side. We gazed at the stars, a bit dazed by the hit, or perhaps the booze. Our fingers were nearly touching.

"You know Cal-bear…" he started to say, "I—"

Tina sat up from the dirty couch. "You two love birds know you are in the dirt right?" She snorted. "Let's bounce, Cal, I'm feeling a bit-" She lurched to the side and started puking into the bushes.

"Oh, shit man," I said, and jumped up to help her.

"Punk ass, let's get you a bed," Joe said.

Joe lifted Tina from the couch after she puked her brains out. But what I really remember from this moment was the way he looked

at me while holding her up. His eyes - blue, deep, and with a hint
of longing.

CHAPTER TEN

I can't believe he's here. I haven't seen him since right after Tina and I graduated college. He stayed in Florida, working full time down there, Tina moved to New York, and I stayed in Pennsylvania, continuing school for my law degree at PITT then later taking the bar exam. Now, our college days now seemed like a lifetime ago. Maybe time really did make the heart grow fonder.

I felt paralyzed when his hand grabbed me, cupping my mouth pulling me into this small dark space. In that moment, I thought I was going to die, that I would suffocate. But just as intensely as I felt about dying, I was excited when I knew it was him. *Cal-bear.* When I heard that nickname, all the pain dissipated. It left me feeling fearful, but for a very different reason.

***

"Shhh" he said.

A sliver of light appeared in the small space as he peered through the horizontal wooden slats on the closet door into the hallway. It was dark in the closet.

"What—what are you doing here?" I say, finally breaking my silence.

"Cal, I… I've been trying to get in touch with–" he starts.

Creaaaaakkk.

Joe places his hand back over my mouth, this time more gently. He looks out again into the hallway.

"You heard that right?" he whispers.

"I have been hearing that sound for two days now," I whisper back. "I have no idea what—"

Creeaaaakk.

Joe moves his hand from my mouth while getting to his feet. I have a feeling he may go to investigate the noise, leaving me in this small, dark closet alone, but I don't want him to leave. He looks into my eyes as if he wanted to tell me something, but just as his full lips part, he turns away and slowly opens the door. "Stay here." he says.

He carefully closes the door behind him. I peek through the slats, watching Joe step toward my bedroom, tip-toing past right Tina and Anthony's room. I notice light underneath their bedroom door again. Joe stops in his tracks. He places his hand on the door handle and slowly turns it… *Creeaaakkkk.* Could the sound have been the handle of that door all along? Joe enters the room. The light turns off and the hallway returns to complete darkness. I can't see anything.

I get to my feet and crack open the closet door.

There is a loud slamming sound and I fall back into the closet. What was that? It was so loud and sudden, as if a tree had fallen on the cabin. *If a tree falls in the forest and no one is around to hear it, does it make a sound?* It made a sound, a very loud and agonizing sound. I push myself back up, pressing my face against the closet door to peek into the hallway. It's still dark. I can't see anything.

I shuffle, inch by inch, toward the room. I press myself against the wall as if to stay hidden in case there is something or someone unfriendly inside. The door is slightly open. The room is dark. My heart is pounding but I can't let something happen to Joe. Especially after… Tina.

I lightly push open the door, placing one foot inside of the room. I have no idea who or what I will find, but I pray to God it's not Joe dead on the floor… My heart is still pounding and I'm sweating now. I press my back against the wall. Something pokes at my back. I turn and feel behind me. It's the light switch. False alarm.

I look around but the room is empty. I try to turn on the light, but it doesn't work. I tiptoe to the bathroom feeling like a silly girl from one of those scary movies again. The room is dark, cold, and… utterly empty. I turn and look at the bed where Tina's purse was left behind, but it's not there. I look and find the small duffle bag in the closet is missing as well. Was someone in the room and took them? I went through her purse earlier and didn't find anything special in it. What could someone have gained by taking it?

My mind starts to wonder again. Maybe Tom took Tina's purse with him when he left? But what reason did he have to remove the purse and the bag? It would have made more sense had it been Anthony who needed it to get Tina's ID from her purse or from the duffle before he left with her. But, thinking back, I don't recall Anthony coming up the stairs before leaving the cabin. The only possible answer is that Tom took all of it.

Where the hell is Joe?

I feel the room spinning around me—but what if Joe took it? He was the last one to enter the room a few moments ago. Maybe all of this was a ploy to get me to trust him, act as if he was the one investigating the scene after we heard a noise, but instead he was the one behind everything. He needed something from the duffle bag. I never thought to open it up to see what was inside. But then again, Tom did somehow disappear into thin air from the cabin just moments before Joe arrived and now Joe was gone too. It all seems too coincidental.

It's a real possibility that I am losing my mind and Joe was really an illusion I created. I shiver at that thought and I run my hands up and down my arms. I remember how I felt when Joe's hand touched mine, when his breath was misting against my neck, when I heard his soft voice say, "*Cal-bear.*" He was here, I know it. I felt it. *Cal-bear*. I couldn't have imagined all of that, could I have?

I make my way to my bedroom at the end of the hallway. The door is wide open, just as I had left it. A chill smacks my face as I enter. The curtains brush the side of my arm. The window is open. Why is the window open? I know I'm not imagining it all now. Someone must have opened it, but who? Was it used to escape from the cabin without being seen?

I think back to the loud slam I heard and wonder if that was the window being opened. Another chill passes through my entire body – from the cold and the fear. I lean over to look out the window and down to the ground while holding on to the sides of the window frame tightly. All I see are mounds of snow jammed along the side of the cabin. But—wait—I take a closer look, squeezing my eyes tightly together as if it would force my vision to improve, but what I see is undeniable even without squinting—*footprints*. One set deeply pressed into the snow and then more leading into the woods. There were no others.

Trying to catch my breath, I quickly pull down the window, slamming it shut and locking it. Whoever was in here and used this window, whether it was Joe, Tom, or anyone else, they-re now long gone now.

***

All of the strange noises have stopped. No more *creaks* or slams or thuds. Only the sound of my own heartbeat.

I return to the first floor and look around but don't see anything changed. Outside the snow has finally stopped falling.

Why is this happening to us? It all seems like a sick joke. Maybe one Joe was playing on all of us just like he used to do with his fraternity brothers back in school. But this feels different, it doesn't *feel* like a joke. It feels like *reality*.

I have no car. Tina's Jag car won't start. I have no phone because there is no signal. I'm totally stranded but not sure if I'm totally alone. I flick on the light switch at the bottom of the stairs. Nothing... now I have no power. Although I had spent the last few hours in the dark anyway, trying to remain unseen, avoiding turning on the lights, now that I know I couldn't turn them on if I wanted, it is suffocating. I'm trapped in a cold cabin in the middle of the woods on the side of a mountain. Far away from everything and everyone with no connection to the outside world or any source of help.

I pace through the kitchen and onto the patio balcony. I look around as if something would suddenly change and Joe would resurface, laughing. *Playing a sick joke.* I would even laugh happily if he reappeared with Tina. "Gotcha," he would say, pointing and laughing at how gullible I had been. But no one appears. No one is laughing.

If possible, the night grows darker, and the cold emptiness more encompassing. Anger rises in me. I run back into the cabin, slamming the balcony door behind me. I am furious. Furious that I have allowed myself to just sit and wait for help to come to me. For answers to somehow walk through the door. I feel like a fool. I am certainly capable of finding my way back to that trail. The signs will lead me to the emergency pavilion to find help and maybe even the others. I need to do something. If I stay here I will either freeze to death or disappear like the rest of them have and I am not willing to just sit around and wait to die.

Quickly making my way to the front entry way, I throw on my thick jacket. I bury my hand in my right pocket confirming my phone is there just in case I ever gain reception. I unlock it but still no bars. No new messages either. Joe must have been the blocked number that texted me earlier based on what he said. Tina's too. Unfortunately, he may know now that he was too late – that Tina is gone. He may have already known it was too late, maybe that is why he came back. Maybe he came back for me. But if he wanted to warn us, why send the messages with a blocked number? What was he hiding or who was he hiding from? And why leave me here abruptly as he did? Unless it wasn't by choice.

I find a pair of thick gloves and put them on. I pull open the door and a gust of wind strikes me. It probably isn't sensible to leave the cabin alone at night and unarmed. But at this point, I have no alternative, I have to find the others. I want to end this nightmare once and for all. I know that I must take the trail up the icy mountain, returning to the deep dark woods to find the answer. To find my friends. To see Joe again.

CHAPTER ELEVEN

Did I miss the turn somehow? Like I did earlier today with Tina? I can barely see my own feet in front of me. Luckily, it wasn't actively snowing anymore, but the wind is knocking down the snow from the pine trees above me.

My eyes sting. I rub them and wipe my face. I'm losing steam from the upward battle and the pervasive numbness. I push forward. I have no alternative. I need to get to the emergency signage to try and find the others. I wasted enough time.

I blink rapidly. A light, not too far ahead of me, reflects off the snow into my eyes. Could it be… Are those…headlights?

Yes! There are two lights side by side up ahead. I push myself harder now. A burst of adrenaline surges through me. I have to hurry. I can't lose sight of whoever this is. They may be my only hope, the only potential contact with another human being. My only way to get out of this God forsaken place.

As I climb harder, faster, up the mountain, the lights don't seem to be moving forward to meet me. I've been moving at a rapid speed towards them, but the lights appear to be still. Is the car stopped?

They're coming from – it can't be—*a green Jeep.* Hysterical now, I run toward it. My legs burn. I wish I had left the cabin sooner. Had they been in an accident? How long had the Jeep has been sitting out here? They must have been coming back towards the cabin. When I reach it, I realize the Jeep is oddly facing the wrong direction. Of course, because the lights were facing me, the cabin.

Maybe there was a blockage further up the mountain, so they were forced to turn back. It's possible, but I don't see any obvious obstructions.

I slip and fall. My left knee scrapes against the ice. I recover and look inside but it's empty. Jesus! Where could they be? Did something happen to them?

I climb into the driver's seat, partly to escape the cold, but mostly to see if they left anything behind. The driver's seat is still warm. They must have just left. I run my hand over the ignition. No keys. More confused than ever, I lean over to look into the back seat. Someone's phone is wedged between the cushions. I turn over and muscle my way into the back to grab ahold of the phone. I don't recognize the phone's case or the image on the lock screen. I can't access any of its contents without a passcode. I slide it into my left pocket and get out of the Jeep.

The snow is settling, forming into thick, slippery ice. This is exactly what I need to make my climb easier. I do a shuffling sidestep towards the emergency sign.

Elva and Anthony must have left the Jeep and made their way for help on foot. I make a right turn at the sign. Suddenly, I feel a vibration in my chest. The buzzing is coming from my left pocket. I pull out the phone I found in the Jeep. The screen lights up and I see "New Message" pop up. I have no way to read it without the code. I don't even know who the phone belongs to to guess. Either Anthony or Elva's most likely since Tina's had been left at the cabin.

Sighing, I start to put it back in my pocket when my eye catches sight of something in the top-right of the screen. A flash of hope run through me. *This phone has reception.* It's showing three bars. I pull out my phone, hoping my access had returned too but no. How does this phone have service and mine does not? I try to dial 911 because the emergency access line should work even if the phone is locked. I hear it try to connect and then immediately disconnect. *Shit.*

Eventually I arrive, out of breath, at a small wooden structure with a tin roof. The cabin shows no indication of life inside. No lights. No sounds. I step up to the front window to peek inside. It looks abandoned. This can't be where the emergency sign was directing me to. I take a moment to catch my breath. I am feeling disoriented and highly discouraged. I walk around the back and find a wooden bench nestled against the wall. Nothing else. I sit. What the hell am I supposed to do now? What was I thinking coming out here alone? Darkness takes over my thoughts. I may die out here.

Faint cries startle me. I jump to my feet, sprinting with renewed energy toward the sound. I can't see anything ahead of me except a deep, dark ditch. Frightened, I take a step closer to the edge. I can't quite make out what I'm seeing. Is that a hand? I shake my head in disbelief but continue staring down into the ditch. Is someone waving for help from the bottom? Without a second thought or the opportunity to overanalyze this chaotic situation, I react. I have nothing to lose. I slide down into the ditch, realizing after doing so that it is several feet deeper than I thought. Its walls are extremely slippery.

"Hello?" I say as I get closer to the bottom. "Is anyone there? Are you alright? I, uh, I can help you." My outstretched hands rub against something smooth, yet sticky. I lift my hand from the dirt wall and find it covered with blood.

"Oh my God!" I scream.

My feet lose traction. I try desperately to wedge them into the sides of the ditch and regain my balance so I can lift my body up. My other hand is placed firmly against the side of the ditch still. Unfortunately, my legs give out and I slip farther down, banging my shoulder against the rocky ground at the bottom.

"Shit!" I yell as I try to lift myself up, then scream in pain as my probably dislocated shoulder moves. I use my other hand to push myself up. I am standing while trying to climb up and out of this hell hole one-handed, but my foot misses a step and I plummet again ground right next to — FUCKING HELL, it can't be – Anthony?

I roll quickly away from the body to the left of me.

"Jesus are you –" I start to ask. But before finishing my sentence, I already know the answer to the question I was going to ask. Of course, he's not okay. How the hell could he be okay? He's not even moving. *Shit.* I don't know why, but I touch his hand to make sure. "Ah!" I shout, jerking away from him. He's definitely dead.

I back up, gripping my shoulder that is now in excruciating pain. I don't know whether to scream bloody murder or cry in despair. Neither will really help me. Instead, I examine the scene. Death was starting to feel like something normal around here. First Tina, now Anthony.

It appears, from the way Anthony fell, that he twisted his arm, probably breaking it. Maybe even breaking his neck as well. His head and palms are both facing upward. Yikes. I'm no medical examiner, but it looks like he might have been pushed rather than falling from a missed step. Could that be? Was Anthony crying out what I heard? But it seemed like he'd been there for quite some time.

I frantically begin to pry my way up and out of the ditch, pushing my feet against the slippery walls, praying to God to give me the strength. I grab the edge, pulling myself out and throwing my body onto the ground above the ditch, leaving Anthony's lifeless body behind me.

"Ouch!" I cry as I again feel my shoulder knocked out of its socket and knowing there is nothing I could do about it right now. I have bigger problems.

I'm trembling both from the cold and from what I just experienced. I can't help but look back down at Anthony lying there dead, alone in a ditch. Sadness comes over me as another life is taken. I didn't know him well and hadn't had the most charitable thoughts about his treatment of Tina, but no one deserved to die like that.

I need to keep moving to stay warm. To find help. Another thought crosses my mind—what if someone is out here watching me? Just waiting to make their next move. I decide my best course of action is to go as fast as I can back to the cabin and hope we find each other again before something else happens.

As I run, as fast as I can clutching my wounded arm to my body, I think about Anthony's pale lifeless face. He had been a handsome man - dark features, tall. My mind switches to Elva. She's likely all alone out here in the dark too. Some person or some animal could attack her. Where is she? Where is Tina's body? What if she's alive? What was Anthony trying to do that that he ended up at the bottom of that ditch?

Out of breath, I kneel. I want to cry, but I know that I can't lose control of myself right now. I need to find Elva, Tom and Joe. I need to find out what is going on. I need to get back to the cabin or I may freeze to death.

I approach the cabin. It's not as welcoming as it once appeared to be. *It reeks of death.* Since the minute each of us walked into the cabin, it has only brought us pain and sorrow. It never brought us closer the way we'd hoped it would. I trudge closer to the door when my left pocket lights up, vibrating against my chest. Another message?

CHAPTER TWELVE

I come back to consciousness. Pain is what I notice first. I reach over to rub my shoulder, but I can't move my arm. I can't move either of my arms. They feel like one-hundred-pound weights have been placed over them, nailing them down to the ground. Panic overtakes me as I realize I can't move my legs either. I try to kick, but my legs feel as if they have been numbed. What is happening to me, why can't I move?

I open my eyes, but I can't see anything. It's dark and wet where I'm lying. My thoughts are foggy, so it takes a moment to realize there's something covering my face. The only thing I can move is my neck, so I rub my face against the rough ground in an attempt to scrape off the cover. It works. I take a deep breath and crane my neck to look down at my body. My hands are tied together with a cream-colored rope and so are my ankles.

I want to scream, but nothing comes out of my mouth. My head is throbbing. It feels like I've been hit by a truck. The pain is excruciating. I must have been hit by something then tied up and thrown here. Wherever here is. I look around me. It resembles the ditch where I found Anthony's corpse. But who put me here and why? Did I know or see too much? Was *I* next?

I think of Tina. Why would someone want to hurt her? I thought her death was an accident, an act of natural causes, maybe from the fall, but somehow now I *know* it wasn't. Then Anthony. And now…*me*? Someone wanted them dead and now they want me dead too. But why? Could we have been unlucky enough to stumble on a serial killer in the woods? It seems unlikely that a serial killer is just here, lingering, waiting for vacationers to strike. It would be more probable that the killer is one of our own. A shiver travels down my back to think that someone I know could be responsible for all of this. Since we arrived, I never saw another soul other than the five of us until Joe randomly appeared. What was he doing here? And those blocked text messages. Why was he so secretive when he sent them? Did he know that someone was going to hurt us? Does he know about Tina? Oh God, Tina, his little sister, my best friend—does he know she's dead?

I continue to struggle, trying to move my arms and legs to free myself from the ropes, but I'm too weak. I try to remember what the last thing was that I did before finding myself in this ditch. I was walking up to the cabin and there was a buzzing light in my pocket. I reached for the phone. Then… nothing. Why the hell am I here? Who put me here? My heart is racing. If the cold doesn't kill me maybe a heart attack will.

A shift above me grabs my attention and I lie completely still. I can hear my heart pounding faster and harder. At least I know that means that I'm still alive. I listen to the sounds above me, telling my thoughts to *"shut the fuck up."* Listening closely might mean life or death.

All I can make out are scrambled sounds. Leaves ruffling in the wind? *Footsteps.* I squint my eyes enough to be able to see but not have them obviously open. It must be… it's definitely footsteps. They're getting closer. I try to breathe shallow, hoping, if it's the killer, they'll think I'm already dead.

***

The sounds stopped. Moonlight no longer reaches the space around me. I feel like I've already been buried. I see nothing, I feel nothing. I might as well be dead. I'm not sure how much time has passed. Maybe only minutes.

My fingers are numb. They may have broken off one by one and I wouldn't feel anything until – my hand trembles. I can feel my hand… I force my brain to wake up, telling it to send any kind of movement to my hand, to awaken it and the rest of my senses. My hand starts to move, my fingers lift from the ground. I feel warmer, my blood pumping through my veins again. I try to shimmy my hands from the rope. My wrists protest in pain, blood coloring the inside of the rope as I finagle my way out. I am grateful to feel anything.

One hand escapes the rope and the other follows. I quickly move down to my ankles, struggling to untie the rope. My legs still feel heavy but are improving. Did the impact from the ditch disable my movements? Did I fall in? I think hard about how I got here but can't remember anything after approaching the cabin. I continue to pull and pry at the rope. I'm free. Not quite Houdini but good enough. I'm woozy and I can't stand up. I look around the ditch, trying to determine the depth of it. Wondering how the hell I am going to get out of here.

In an excited panic, I pat at my jacket, remembering the two phones. There's nothing in my pockets now. Someone must have found the phones on me and taken them. Someone clearly does not want me to contact anyone. I need to get myself together and pull myself out of this hole or I will die out here.

"Shhh."

I hear a sound so light and airy that I wonder if it was a part of my imagination. I stop moving and hold my breath. This is it… whoever, whatever it is has returned to make sure I was finished off.

"Cal?" I hear a man call for me.

I'm saved! My heart is beating with excitement now rather than fear. If it was a serial killer surely, he wouldn't have known my name.

"Down here!" I scream.

Footsteps approach the ditch, first slowly, then picking up speed. I try to stand, but lose my balance, looking upward.

"Hang on," my rescuer says as a rope is thrown down, nearly hitting me. "Do you see it?"

"Um, yes, barely, but I feel it. Who's there?"

"It's Tom"

Tom? The last time I saw him was inside the cabin right before – well right before he disappeared along with Joe. He was piss drunk, so I am not sure where he'd gone, perhaps stumbled out into the forest to pass out amongst the trees? Well, he was here now, helping me out and I was going to take it. That has to count for something, right?

"You alright? I'm going to pull you up. Hang on tight!"

I cling to the rope, wrapping the end around my waist.

"Ready?" he asks.

"Yes, pull!" I yell back.

The rope starts to move toward an incline and upward. I grip it tightly, screaming out in agony as my shoulder is jostled along with the rest of my nearly beaten body. I can feel the rope cutting into the skin of my hands. God help me get through this, I think as I grip tightly, my blood coloring the rope.

Suddenly, I find myself above ground. With another few pulls, I land, striking my injured shoulder. It's painful but the alternative was much worse.

"Tom! Thank you" I cry.

I can't believe he's here. That I'm out of the ditch.

***

I wake up again inside a warm car, reclining in the front passenger seat. My skin registers soft leather. I look over and see Tom driving.

"There you are." he says with a smirk. "I thought we'd lost you there for a second."

I'm glad to see a familiar face, one that is alive and well.

"I can't thank you enough. I have no idea what happened, how I ended up there," I say confused but aware enough to study Tom's expression.

He looks sympathetic, worried, and mostly sincere. I watch his hand as it turns the knob to turn up the heat. "Are you warm enough?" he asks as he keeps his hand on the temperature dial.

"Compared to where I was, anything is better," I reply trying to make light of the traumatic situation. I rub my shoulder, looking down at my bloody hands, then around the vehicle. We're inside Elva's Jaguar.

I'm surprised. The last time I tried to turn the ignition on in this car it failed to start. I'd tried to tell Tom the Jag didn't work back at the cabin, but when I returned inside, he was gone. How did he start the car? I look at his face, again. He seems to be concentrating. I look out the front windshield but it's difficult to see. It's still pitch black outside. Although, at this point, it has to be in the early morning hours. I look for a clock on the car's dash but catch Tom's eye and quickly look away. Only the headlights of the vehicle guide us. I hope Tom can see better than I can.

"Where is Elva?" I finally ask, breaking the silence. Tom doesn't answer. I repeat the question a bit louder, thinking he didn't hear me.

"Don't you worry, darling. You are going to be just fine." he says.

I sit back, my heart racing as fast as it was when I first heard the muffled footsteps approach the ditch. I was excited then, in my eagerness to escape from the ditch, but again something isn't right. How did Tom know I was in that ditch in the first place? And why is he ignoring my question now? I want to know where the hell is Elva.

Despite my concerns, I sit quietly, observing the road. I finally see white lines confirming we are on a paved road. I look at the cup holder, seeing the medicine bottle I put there after finding it under the seat of the driver's seat earlier. The cap looks slightly elevated. I look up to see if Tom is looking in my direction. But he's not.

"Are we heading back to the cabin?" I ask nervously.

Could Tom have killed Elva? Is that why he is ignoring my questions? Because if he killed her, he probably killed Tina and Anthony. And plans to take me out as well? But if he intended to kill me, why come back to help me out of the ditch? Why not just leave me there to die?

I look over at him. He's smirking.

"Yes, we are almost there. Sit tight, darling."

It occurs to me that is the second time he's called me "darling." I look over at the passenger door and consider pulling the handle and rolling out. Hitting the ground while the wheels are in motion would be excruciatingly painful but what if I got caught under the back wheels or landed wrong and died out there trying to escape dying in here?

We should have been back at the cabin by now. But then I had no concept of where exactly the ditch I was in was located. It just *feels* like too long of a ride.

The car comes to a stop and Tom immediately exits, leaving me locked in the passenger seat. I watch him as he walks around the vehicle to the passenger side. He opens my door and I look up at him. His face is cold and expressionless. I feel my heart about to exit my throat.

"Get out," he says as he holds the door open.

This is it; I am now at my end. And I'd thought it was the ditch.

Tom closes the door behind me. My mind starts to race as fast as my heart. Of course, Tom is the murderer. He was a bit too nice of a guy all along. It's always the good ones that you miss seeing the signs in, right? I mean, how could someone who is uninvolved locate me in a random, dark ditch in the middle of the woods?

But it leaves so many other questions unanswered. What would motivate Tom to do this? His love for Elva had always blinded him to a fault, but whatever he did he did it of his own free will. He chose the life that he has with her. He's the only man that was able to nail Elva down anyway, have a child with her and marry her. What could possibly cause him to turn into a monster, to kill her friends? He may have killed her too! I think about their daughter, Flora, who is so young and beautiful just like her mother. She has an entire life in front of her not knowing her father is a cold-blooded murderer.

As I take step after step, I observe my surroundings, but see nothing familiar. Finally, Tom leads me to a small wooden house that looks very familiar to me.

"Tom—where are the others?" I built up the courage to ask.

"It will all make sense," he says as he guides me through the door.

I reluctantly enter, looking at it from the inside out.

Tom leads me to sit, placing a pillow behind my lower back and head. I don't say a word. I'm watching him closely, at least what I can see of him in the dark room. The place is approximately the size of a shoebox for better lack of measurement. Before the door closed behind me, all I could see was the small bench I'm now seated on, a sink and a small cabinet in the corner. There don't appear to be any windows.

"Here, drink this, you'll need it to stay hydrated." Tom hands me a glass. I take the glass but don't drink.

"Don't worry, just drink it – *trust me*," he says as he lifts the glass to my mouth, encouraging me to consume all of its contents.

Trust me. The words ring in my ears. How the hell can I trust you when you're acting so suspiciously and won't tell me what's going on. What choice do I have? I could scream, try to run, but to where? I have nowhere to go. I don't even know where I am. I've already escaped death what feels like multiple times in one day. Surely this time I wouldn't be so lucky. I hold the glass up to confirm that its contents are clear. My mouth waters at just the thought of drinking it. I am so very thirsty. But something inside of my gut tells me not to. What if he's trying to poison me?

Tom stands over me aggressively, pushing between my knees. He presses the glass against my mouth.

"Drink it."

This time I obey and empty its contents.

CHAPTER THIRTEEN

I open my eyes, it should be daylight by now surely, but there isn't enough light to tell. The only light comes from the crack at the bottom of the door. I rub my eyes and sit up. I was slouched back in a pillow against the wall with the bench underneath me. I am nauseated. I reach for the glass of water but it's empty. I try to stand, but the room spins. I felt the same way when I woke up in the ditch. There is a pull at my ankles when I try to stand again.

I'm chained to the wooden bench. Trapped again. I look around the dim room but all I see are a coat and keys in the opposite corner from me. I recognize the jacket as being Tom's but he's nowhere in sight. I pull at the chain on my ankle. Then I try to lift the bench to release it but won't budge. The bench is attached to the floorboards somehow. I look around again, this time to find anything I can use to break the chain. There's nothing in reach but the glass next to me. Without thinking, I break the glass, holding its base to keep it from completely shattering. My hands are still torn and bleeding from the rope. Glass shards fly all around the room. I use the base to chip at the wooden bench, creating a dent in the wood, sawing at the same spot over and over again hoping it will eventually weaken and allow me to release the chain underneath it. I feel woozy. My stomach unsettled, growling from hunger. I feel like I haven't eaten in ages. I have completely lost track of time.

The doorknob turns. I stop what I'm doing and hide the glass shard behind me, sitting on it slightly. The piece stabs into my bottom, but I need to make sure I can defend myself. The doorknob turns and the door opens. A light silhouettes around a tall man walking into the cabin. Glass cracks under his feet as he moves toward me. Is it Tom coming back to finish me off? I fist the glass in my hand, readying to strike.

He stops.

Joe?

***

He breaks the leg of the bench and releases my ankle from the chains. I take his hand and we rush outside. Without words, we half-run half-hobble into the woods. The wind grazes my face for the first time in days as we make our escape.

My hand gripping Joe's, I feel safe for the first time. *Trust me.* I think back to what Tom said as I drank the contents of my glass. I woke to find myself confined once again, chained like an animal. So now I hold Joe's hand and flee from Tom, but in fear of what lies ahead. Can I trust Joe? I really want to. I know him well. He may be the only hope I have to get out of these woods.

His hand is thick, cupping mine. I want to say so many things to him, but I can't. I want to ask him what happened to him in the cabin and if he's hurt, but I remain silent. His hand squeezes mine as we walk deeper, pushing aside tree branches and bushes in our path. The ground is wet and soggy. Our feet sink into it with every step. My arms are covered with goosebumps, and we struggle to keep our balance as wind gusts hit us. The moon fades until the darkness is the only thing we can see.

Joe grips harder, tighter, to make sure we do not lose each other again. I trust him. I have to trust him. I'm out of my element, in horror of what has happened to all of us. I still have no idea what Tom did with Elva. Is she still alive? And if so, where is she? Is she hurt? Did he chain her somewhere just like he chained me? Drugged us both? Is that why I blanked out, why I can't remember anything? Is that how he tied me up and threw me in a ditch only to rescue me, drug me, and then chain me up again? What kind of sick fuck does that? Why kill Tina and Anthony? How? I can't allow the thoughts to overtake me. We have to keep moving to survive.

I look at Joe as we walk hand in hand. The night doesn't allow me to make out his expression, but I think he looks determined. He saved me from a maniac, twice now. Who knows what Tom's plans were for me? I was lucky to get out. I was lucky Joe found me. I smile, but my smile turns to a melancholy frown. *Joe.* It's odd how he's always around at just at the right time. Just when everything is going wrong. Saving the day, coming out of nowhere like a knight in shining armor.

I start to pant. Joe looks at me with concern. I nod to signal I'm okay, but in my head, I am at a dead stop. He is always there. *Cal-bear.* I recall him saying as he lifted his hand off my mouth, after what nearly felt like he was suffocating me. He is always there, in the right place at the right time. My heart starts to pound again. I think he could tell I was panicking, maybe he felt my heartbeat through my hand.

"It's okay, we just need to get a bit further," he says as he pulls me forward by the hand.

Cal-bear, Cal-bear, CAL-BEAR! The words run through my mind in a panic. What if Joe is behind all of this? What if he orchestrated this entire trip around eliminating each of us, one by one? But why his own sister? They never were enemies. And then where did Tom fit in? It doesn't add up. But the text messages… Was he warning us or covering something up? If Joe sent the text messages to Tina and I, why send them blocked? We had no reason not to trust him. Was he trying to hide something from us or from the others? Could he have been in the house when Tina was unconscious? Is that why he's reacting like this, thinking we hurt her?

No. The only person I have reason to fear at the moment is certainly not Joe, the one that saved me. Tom is the one to fear.

It starts to rain hard and heavy. We hunch over as we walk, but it's useless. We are drenched and we can't see two feet in front of ourselves between the rain and the dark. Joe slips downward in a rivulet along the side of the cliff. He let's go of my arm so he won't pull me down with him. I yell as if that would help stop him. I watch in horror as he slides down the cliff.

"Joe!" I yell as I make my way down carefully to him.

His back slams against a tree. As I struggle to reach him, I feel every ounce of regret that I doubted him. I need to make sure he's okay. I can immediately see that he's hurt. His leg is slightly bent in what appears to be the opposite direction from the rest of his body but he's conscious. He was lucky the water didn't take him off the cliff. I sit next to him under the giant pine tree that stopped his fall, probably saving his life.

"Joe, you're going to be alright," I say, not knowing whether either of us actually will be alright.

I touch his stubbled face. His eyes are tired. He takes my hand and holds it tightly.

"Cal-bear, I... it was a mistake to leave you behind, I'm sorry, I was conflicted," he starts as my eyes meet his, "but, more than anything, I want you to know..."

I look deeper into his eyes, light turning their blue to a shade of gray. "I love you," he says as he inches closer to me, pressing his lips to mine.

I move closer to him, pressing our bodies closer to keep us from freezing in this cold, wet, dark place.

CHAPTER FOURTEEN

Seconds turn to minutes, minutes turn to hours, hours turn to what feels like days—days long and cold as we wait for someone to find us, to get us both out of this Godforsaken place. Joe's leg is definitely broken. He can't even stand up, so walking on it is out of the question.

I want to break out of this nightmare and return to my normal, boring life of endless pleadings, disgruntled clients, and virtual court hearings. But I realize that this experience has changed me, and that I really could never really be *normal* again. I lost my best friend, but I gained someone to live for - Joe. But we need to survive this first.

As if on cue, sirens wail in the distance. I watch in disbelief as a helicopter flies over the trees above us. We wait. Our frost-bitten fingers still gripping one another. I've let go of him too many times to do it again. Part of me feels I could lie here indefinitely while the other part of me knows if we stay any longer we'll die of hypothermia. The wind from helicopter blades beats around us as it gets closer, setting down on the rocky edge of the steep cliff. I look at it with hope and gratitude. We are going to make it out of this nightmare, finally.

A man, geared up in official-like attire resembling that of a search and rescue party, peeks out of a wide opening on the side of the helicopter. I read the acronym "AMRG" on a patch sewn and placed on the man's left pocket's uniform. His headset and eyes are covered as he yells over in our direction. I cannot hear anything from the blazes slicing into the wind, muting our ears.

My sight, hearing and other senses are all minimized. The helicopter inches even closer to us, as the man rests one foot on the mountain's edge and his other still in the helicopter. A second man leaps out of the helicopter to assist him. They strategically place Joe on a stretcher lifting him into a dark compartment onboard the helicopter. "Can you take my hand?" one of the men asks as they reach out to me, "Are you injured?" he asks further as he prepares to send for a second stretcher to assist me. I shake my head, my mouth is so dry and cold I cannot speak, but before I could even respond, the second man is loading me unto a second beige stretcher and lifting me into the helicopter securely next to Joe.

I look around the interior of the helicopter compartment as I am stabilized by a tall man hunched over in uniform. Questions race through my mind. How did they find us? How did they even know to look for us? Did they find any of the others? I think back to the call I made from the phone with service, maybe that call went through.

I build up the nerve to ask, "how did you find us?"

"Roger, we are on the way to the hospital" the man reports to someone through his headset. He fails to respond to my question. I am not sure he even heard it. Not surprising from the blazes slicing over us.

"They are stable—over" he reports again as we fly over the tall pines where we once sat below. I watch from the opening as we turn away from the deep dark woods.

***

I wake to the smell of a sterilized room. I'm dizzy, tired, and in shock. I look around but I'm alone. Joe? Where is Joe? I have no idea where I am. Confusion and panic set in. But I am quickly greeted by a petite woman wearing scrubs.

"Calista, I'm Nurse Mederin. You're in Allegheny General Hospital. The Allegheny Mountain Rescue Group brought you in." She says and continues "You have suffered a severe case of frostbite."

I try to jump up, but she pushes me back down against the bed. "…Lie back, you're okay. As I was saying, generally, we would say someone who has been out in the cold for the duration we have calculated that you may have would have been fatal case, however you are one very fortunate young lady." She smiles.

I blink looking at the nurse, smiling and thankful to be out of the woods *alive*.

The nurse conducts a cognitive assessment. "Please confirm your full name and date of birth" she requests as she stands by with a pen and paper attached to her clipboard as if to check items off a list.

"Calista Jokovic, October 13, 1987." She quickly checks off the paper in front of her as I respond.

"What year is it?" She says and continues "Tell me anything you remember as to why you and um—why you were out where AMRG found you?"

"It's 2024. Um—" I start but am hesitant to say too much. I have no intention of incriminating the others, especially since I have no information as to why this is all happening. I feel like I can't trust anyone right now.

"We were out hiking" I say, "We must have gotten lost in the woods. Joe had fallen, injuring himself."

I watch as her jot down a few too many things on her clipboard and unclick her pen.

I can finally relax. I'm in a hospital and in good hands, right? However, my ease is short lived. There is more to the story than the nurse may be aware of. I look out towards the door expecting police officers to come in and question me but see no one in sight waiting. Surely someone will look to question me about what happened to Tina, to Anthony… to the rest of us. I am not out of the woods quite yet.

"In addition, you fractured your left shoulder. Surgery was successful. We anticipate you will have full range and motion in about six to eight weeks," the nurse says with another smile. "You will be just fine." She winks at me and closes her clipboard in front of her.

"My – friend…" I start before the nurse interrupts.

"Oh yes, Joseph Williams, is that him? Well, he was brought into the hospital by trauma at the same time you arrived."

"Is he… he is okay? Can I see him?" I ask.

"He wasn't as lucky as you my dear. He will need to stay a few nights for observation as he severely fractured his right leg. He's currently in surgery. Is he your husband, boyfriend?" the nurse asks, eyeing me while opening the clipboard back up, clicking her black ink pen to note my response.

"He is my um — friend, actually my boyfriend," I say with some hesitation. "Is he okay?" I ask again, more panicked than the first time but hoping she will give up more information.

"He will be. Because you're not family, I am sorry, but I can't give you any additional details. You understand. I may have said too much already…" she says, securing the flap over the clipboard once again and checking my vitals.

"Is there someone we can call for you? Maybe for your friend as well, a family member perhaps?" she asks as she checks my blood pressure and pulse.

Who would she call for me? My mother would only panic, I cannot put her through that. I think about Tina. I wonder if Joe even knows that Tina is dead. Not sure what other family member information I could give the nurse to contact on his behalf? Tina's mother for one, but that is about it. How could I face her and tell her about Tina?

I shake my head.

"You sure? Someone is going to have to drive you home once you're released. You can't drive yourself with that shoulder." She points to my wrapped shoulder in a sling. "… and the zolpidem in your system…" she says, continuing to check my vitals and make additional notes on the white clipboard.

An electric shock jolts through my body as I realize what the nurse said.

"Excuse me?"

She looks over at me as if I am insane. "The zolpidem…" she stays as she rolls her eyes, "…it may help explain how you got to the edge of the cliff."

She must realize she may have overstepped. "What I mean, is — perhaps some of the side effects of your medicine may have made you feel a bit…tired, unable to walk straight, that's all…" she says trailing off as she walks out.

The nurse thinks that the prescription is mine.

I feel a massive migraine coming on. My heart pounds from anger. Tom obviously left the cabin to find Elva and Anthony only to make sure that Tina never saw the light of day again, that no help would reach any of them. But why Elva? He longed for her. He would have done anything for her. Maybe he snapped, tired of being her pet, her yo-yo yanked up and down over and over again. He'd pleaded with her to work a bit less, spend time with the family, with Flora, be a mother to their daughter, but she refused. Maybe he felt that she belittled him as a man, as her husband. Maybe he was the one that wanted to take control for once.

It all makes sense now why Tom acted the way he did… pretending to be drunk, passing out on the sofa in the cabin. Pretending to be worried about Tina. Only to leave as soon as I turned my back. He must have drugged Tina, that's why she fell and seemed out of it on the hike. Then he gave her enough to knock her out permanently so he could force us out of the house only to come after us later, killing us, one at a time. *Trust me.* The words replay in my mind. I was a fool to trust him. He wanted us all dead.

But what about Joe? He rode in like a knight in shining armor. But just as quickly as he came, he disappeared into thin air. How did he even get to the cabin? There were no other vehicles parked in the driveway, at least none that I saw. I lean back into my hospital bed, slowly this time to make sure I don't hurt my shoulder. *Cal-bear. Cal-bear. I love you…* I take a deep breath. I felt something for Joe then and, if I was honest with myself, I had for a long time. He was the only guy that ever took my breath away. His laugh flooded my soul. But he was Tina's brother, and I didn't feel right to do that to her even though I adored everything about him. But *could I trust him?* Where was he when he left the closet in the cabin? He walked out into Tina and Anthony's room only to disappear just like Tom did. He never explained himself. The window was open. I remember the freezing air coming through it that night as I stood looking out. I remember seeing footsteps leading into the forest. *Cal-bear.* How can I trust him? How can I trust anyone?

***

I was awakened by a woman's voice outside of my room. She was talking about a patient at the hospital. I couldn't hear her clearly, but I knew it wasn't about me. They kept referring to the mystery patient as a "her", saying she was fragile, weak, and thin. But then I hear more—how she was brought to the hospital by a couple, who dropped her off and left quickly. I slowly inch myself to sit up. I need to hear who the nurses are talking about, but their voices start to fade until they walk out of earshot. It could have been about anyone. Right?

The nurse returns with her clipboard and a fake smile on her face. She checks my vitals once again as I sit in silence, not sure what to say or ask her. I have so many questions, but I also fear that asking her may somehow incriminate myself. "Mmhm, very good. Looks like you are due for a release in the next day or so young lady. I need to check with the doctor, but everything is checking out quite nicely," she says.

Although from the look in her eyes I could see something more. As if she could tell what I was thinking, how I was feeling, like she knew something was wrong. I nod. I should be happy to get the hell out of here. Go home.

"Is Joe—Joseph Williams, still here?" I ask the nurse.

She raises an eyebrow. She takes pity on me. We did come into the hospital together after all. "He is doing just fine, don't you worry," she says as she pats my shoulder lightly, "he will be alright, I promise."

"And the others?" I ask as the nurse raises an eyebrow.

"The others?" she repeats. She must think I am losing my mind. I had never mentioned Tina, Elva, Tom or Anthony or anyone else to her since I got to the hospital.

"Yes, um—my friends. We were hiking with other friends" I lie as I watch Nurse Mederin reopen her clipboard and click her black pen.

"Ok tell me about the others" she says and waits.

"Well, there were four others—" I stop myself "sorry two others." I don't want to tell her about Anthony and Tina's corpse since she may get the police involved. I am not trying to incriminate myself here, I know better.

"Ok, so two others" she repeats as she scratches out and rewrites something on the clipboard in front of her.

I instantly feel that mentioning the others was a mistake as I have no actual foundation as to where they may be, what their involvement is in this entire thing and who I can trust. I worry that Tom may be out there running wild like some kind of psycho serial killer. I do want to protect Elva. *If she is still alive.* But I can't, I must protect myself now.

"Go on..." the nurse says impatiently tapping the black pen on the clipboard.

"I'm sorry. I'm not sure. I still feel a bit foggy" I lie.

Her eyebrows peak "I see..." she says as she notates something else on the clipboard and closes it. "Get some rest."

She leaves, closing the door behind her.

CHAPTER FIFTEEN

The anxiety of the weekend follows me as I hurry to unlock the top deadbolt, my hands trembling. I wave back to Jerry to thank him for bringing me home. I push open the door to find everything exactly as I had left it. Mr. Whiskers purrs as I run my hand over his soft silky head. His tail rises and falls as he walks through my hand and jumps up on my desk next to the door. It's only been a few days, but it feels like weeks. I walk over to grab a garbage bag and empty out the litter box. Shivering, I turn up the heat.

I double-knot the garbage bag, returning the litter box to its station. Mr. Whiskers purrs and rubs against me as if saying thank you for finally coming home and taking care of this mess mom. I hesitate but open the front door letting the cold chill enter the now warm house as I drag out the garbage. I have never wanted winter to end as badly as I do now.

I remember that I need to see if I've received a response to my motion. I filed it prior to leaving for the trip. The latch on the mailbox takes some force to open because of ice around the metal rim. There are a few standard white envelopes and a small package from USPS. Unfortunately, there is no manilla envelope, so likely no reply to my filing.

I run back into the house, closing and locking the door behind me. I readjust my sling. The pain is excruciating after the surgery, but the pain medicine helps Mr. Whisker's has settled back into his bed, snoozing away without a care in the world. It's nice to be home. I throw down the envelopes and open the box. I didn't order anything. The sender's address is not listed, only my own. Curious, I unfold its cardboard flaps. Inside is a single piece of paper. Folded in half and taped shut. I see something underneath it but decide to tear open the note first.

"Hold this for me." No signature. Nothing else.

I reach into the box, shifting the tissue paper filler, and my hands hits something. I pull it out.

"Holy shit!" I scream as I find a medicine bottle. I turn the label to read its contents and drop the bottle, cupping my hand over my mouth.

***

Reluctantly, I pick up the note and read it again as if I had missed something reading it the first time. *"Hold this for me."* Did Elva send me the package with the bottle? Unfortunately, I can't make out who's handwriting it is. Could it be the nurse from the hospital, but no—it couldn't have been her, she never had the bottle, and she would never have asked me to hold it for her. Jesus—was it from Tom? Was he trying to hide the bottle or frame me somehow? But why would he send it to me to "hold it" for him, does that mean he would be back to retrieve it from me? I turn around making sure the lock is deadbolted on the front door. Then I check the rest of the room for open windows or doors. Everything looks secure. My nightmare from the past few days is far from over and someone is purposely trying to keep me involved.

My housephone rings.

"Everything check out?" a man's voice asks. I shake off my nerves for a second to realize it's Jerry.

I don't want to alarm him, he has heart problems as it is, and the last thing I need to do is to involve him in any of this. "Jerry—thank—you, I... I'm fine, all good, thanks for the ride back."

"Calista, you should have called me sooner, what happened to you out there?"

It's not too often that someone goes on vacation with their friends, ends up in the hospital with a broken shoulder, gets drugged, and returns alone with no word if the friends are dead or alive.

"Look, Jerry, I'm fine. Thank you for your concern. I'm going to rest up and get back to it Tuesday morning."

"Alright Cal, you get your rest, I need you in tip-top shape for that hearing next week," he says and hangs up. Of course, it all boils down to work for Jerry. As much as we're friendly, I still work for the guy. He may be concerned for my wellbeing—and I do believe he cares—he puts work ahead of everything else.

I turn over the package a few times to make sure I didn't miss anything. I turn to flip my own bag over but realize I don't have it. I must have lost it at some point while searching for the others. frantically pull out everything inside to make sure there are no surprises in it. Turning to find my jacket, I frantically pat it and myself down to make sure there are no surprises. My cellphone is missing. I try to recall the last place I saw it but cannot remember. It must still be in my jacket. I wanted to call Elva, to ask her about the mailing, to explain herself, to explain the medicine and why she was prescribed it to begin with. The problem is I cannot remember anyone's phone number. I used to know Elva's, Tina's, and my mom's phone numbers by heart, now all I can remember is my mom's number. All the others are stored in my cellphone. Which I do not have. *Great.*

I open my laptop to access my email account. Luckily, all my photos, numbers, and the like are saved on the cloud. I scroll down to "E" and jot down the number on the back of the note from the package. I'm relieved I never disconnected the housephone. Most people did these days. I may be the only person I can think of that still has a housephone. But it's been convenient to call it my "office line" so clients can think I actually have a proper office.

I dial out. The phone rings, but no one picks up. Elva disappeared with Anthony, and the way Anthony ended up, Elva could very well be six feet under somewhere too. I try to shake the thought out of my mind. I don't want to believe it. I need to know what happened to her and to Anthony, and what in the hell they did with Tina's body. It's as if Tina and Elva vanished.

I try dialing out again and wait. Suddenly, the ringing stops and there is silence. I wait—then wait a bit longer. More silence.

"Hello?"

The line disconnects and all I hear is dial tone. I start to feel the same twisting and turning that I felt many times over the past couple of days. Nothing makes sense. Why would Elva pick up and not say "hello?" I dial again. Someone picks up, but again there is no greeting.

"Elva, please, if that's you say something. It's Cal. I need to know that you're okay." As soon as it came out of my mouth the phone line disconnects. *Shit.*

Almost at the same moment, I hear a *ding* from my laptop. I got an email.

The subject reads: *I am sorry.*

The sender, *ElvaBronson@gmail.com*

What the fuck is going on? I need to know what happened to her. I open the email. The interior is blank. The subject line is the message. *I am sorry…* the words run through my head on repeat. She's sorry for what? For not answering the call, for sending the medicine unaddressed, for disappearing pretending to be *dead?*

Ding

You have one unread message.

Another email? This time the subject line is blank.

To: CalistaJokovic@gmail.com

From: ElvaBronson@gmail.com

Come back.

Come back… Come back to where? To the cabin. For a lack of better words, over my dead body, but I feel like I have no other choice. What's the alternative? Stay here, alone, and wonder what has happened to her, Tina, Anthony? What if something happens to me? No one would ever know. I didn't tell Jerry or the nurse anything. As far as I knew, Joe was in the hospital waiting to be released. I never had Joe's number so I can't call him. No one knows anything about the cabin, the trail, Tina, Anthony… no one but me and whoever is on the other end of this email. I have no choice but to go. I grab my keys and walk out the door.

CHAPTER SIXTEEN

The weather is the same as we left it, dreary. Though the snow had melted away, and the rain finally stopped. A chill pass through me just thinking about being back in this hell hole. I thought about turning back a few hours along the drive, but I knew I was left with no choice if I wanted any answers.

The driveway is empty. The cabin is dark, no visible lights on inside. I immediately regret not bringing a weapon for protection. Not that I have a gun or even something like a crowbar or baseball bat. I look in the back seat of my car to see if there was anything I could use in a pinch. I only find a small black umbrella. Good enough. I retrieve it, placing it under my arm in my jacket.

I shut the engine off and wait. I wait for some kind of signal to indicate that Elva is waiting for me inside. After all, she was the one that told me to return. But the longer I sit and wait for some kind of movement, the more I don't see or hear anything. My nerves start to get the best of me. I'm worried I might vomit. I swallow the bile rising up at my thoughts. I take a deep breath and get out of the car.

I slowly make my way up the steps to the front entry. The wooden bear still awaits, but this time he doesn't seem as friendly. It's as if its expression has been remolded, reflecting anger, resentment, and horror. I am going insane. I get closer to the door, step by step, anticipating the worst. Nothing good has come from this cabin. I look behind me to see if someone is behind me. No one is there. I get chills at the thought. I know that I'm freaking myself out.

I stand in front of the door, peering inside through its stained-glass. Should I ring the bell, knock, or just open it? I turn the nob. The door is unlocked. I push and it creaks open as if it hadn't been opened in years instead of days. I force myself to take a step inside, hoping to find Elva sitting on the couch. Maybe she would run over and greet me in her old bubbly kind of way.

I walk further into the cabin. "Hello, anyone here?" I finally ask as I look around, flicking on the light switch. The lights flicker on once, twice, and then stay off. The storm must have knocked the power out or a fuse blew. The room is so cold I can see my own breath in front of me.

"Elva?" I call out, as I continue to walk through the cabin toward the back patio. The same place where drinks were shared, and cigarettes were smoked that first night. I push open the door to the outside and look out remembering the footsteps in the snow below heading in the direction of the woods. Thinking about the open window in my room upstairs.

Light beams through the window. I go back inside and see its from headlights shining through the front window. A vehicle is pulling into the driveway. I walk to and try to peek out but can't see clearly because the lights are blinding in the dark. After a few moments, the headlights turn off. I can feel my heart beating back into my throat. Keys jingle as someone takes one, two, three steps up to the landing in front of the door. I take a step back, and then a few more, backing away from whoever is coming. Keys rattle in the lock before they realize it is already unlocked. The nob turns and the door is pushed open.

I grip the small black umbrella under my right arm like a lifeline. Hoping that I will have no use for it. In enters — *Tina*.

***

To say I'm in shock is an understatement as I stare into the big brown I eyes I thought I would never see again. How is she here? She was basically *dead*; I saw it with my own two eyes. I thought that I felt her pulse with my two fingers when I touched her cold lifeless body on the very sofa we are both now standing next to. It felt like hours passed before Anthony and Elva took her to seek help that day. How could she have been alive? It did not even seem like she was breathing. But as impossible as it may seem, she's standing right in front of me now, very much alive. I want to slap myself to make sure I'm not hallucinating. Have I gone completely mad?

"Tina—how—is… is that you—but how I thought you were…" I stammer as I try to say what we are both thinking.

You were dead, I know you were, you were in front of me, in front of all of us, lifeless, dead, you were *dead*. This is impossible. I want to run over to her and wrap both of my arms tightly around her waist in excitement, but I stop myself. This isn't right. I take a few steps back. The darkness in the room is too thick to see her face clearly even with the moonlight.

"Tina?"

"Maybe you should sit down," she says.

I have the urge to faint, to panic in disbelief. I take a few steps back towards the sofa. My calves hit the front of the sofa. The same sofa where Tina laid dead days ago. I fall back onto it.

"But how, how are you here? You were dead!"

I can now see her face clearly now, she's at just the right angle for what light there is to catch her features.

She gave an unfriendly smirk. Any feeling of excitement I had faded. I may be having a heart attack. I can't catch my breath without deeply inhaling. I'm breaking out in a cold sweat.

"You were all so very quick to rid of me, weren't you?" she says, stepping directly in front of my knees.

I'm trembling now at the thought of what is next. What will she do with me? Why am I here? I shift to the left and mirrors me as if to block me from standing up.

"Ti—tina, I..." I say, my voice shaking. "I thought you were dead."

She looks at me coldly. "Well, I'm not," she says.

"I felt for your pulse. Your heart wasn't beating."

She says nothing.

"Did you—" I start to speak again but come to realization that there was no chance in hell she knew I would be here *unless she invited me here.* But how would she have had access to Elva's email? Oh my God, she has Elva's phone. But then what happened to Elva?

I need to tread lightly I'll end up like Anthony, or maybe like Elva, wherever she is. But why would she do that to him? To Elva? What does she want to do to me?

"Did I *what* Calista?" she says mockingly. *Calista*, no Cal or *Cali*. She was fucking with me. She knew what she'd done and now she was going to do it to me.

"All of you with your fucking stupid jokes. You have no idea what I've been through, what we have been through!" she says, her eyes look wide and wild.

What did she mean by your jokes? Who the hell was laughing at her? No one said shit to her about anything. And I was the sympathetic one when she told me about her and Anthony splitting up. When she cried over her miscarriage. How could any of us have done something to her? We hadn't spoken to or seen each other in forever. This was supposed to be a reunion, to catch up, to relax, to enjoy each other's company. I know now what she'd been through, and I was supportive when she told me about it. Why bring me here? To what end? To confront me, to surprise me, show me that she'd escaped death somehow and get rid of me? The more I look at her, the less she looks like herself. The Tina I knew in college, the girl that let loose every so often, who partied in the sorority and frat houses, who took swigs of whiskey in the back of her brother's truck. She's nothing like that girl now. She is filled with rage, anger, and bitterness.

I don't want to believe she would ever hurt me. But her eyes... they are dark and dangerous, she's possessed.

"I completely understand where you are coming from Tina, we—I was wrong to have joked around—you know I take you seriously," I say in an attempt to be soothing.

She backs away a bit and grips her head with both hands. "Ughh, I had to, Cal. He was going to leave me!" she shrieks, throwing both of her hands down and sitting next to me.

I need to be calm so that she can be calm. Pretend I'm comfortable with this insane conversation. As much as I want to run out the door, I know I can't. I need to see this through. I need to know what she did with Elva and if there is still hope of helping her.

I place one hand over Tina's and inch closer to her on the sofa. She looks up at me as if her first instinct was to throw my hand off, but she doesn't move away.

"I know how you feel" I reply, but even to my ears that sounds stupid. I don't know anything about what she's going through, I haven't faked my death and killed all of my friends. But I have to play this cool until I can figure out what to do next. Maybe Elva actually was coming to the cabin, maybe it really was her that sent the email. I need to hold out.

"How could you know how I feel Cal? I was supposed to be a mother. We were supposed to get married. He fucked everything up!" Her volume escalates with her anger.

I grip her hand tighter. "It's not your fault. It seems like you had your reasons." I don't know what to say to a psychopath. Just the memory of finding Anthony down in the ditch... I'm horrified that one of my best friends was capable of doing something like that, regardless of what kind of asshole he may have been. Being a jerk shouldn't equal a death sentence.

She squeezes my hand back. Her face lightens and she starts to cry. It seems sincere. "You think I wanted to be like this? I wanted to be married, raise children, work part time. There is so much pressure from all ends. It wasn't supposed to end up like this. I just wanted him to see what it was like to not have me…" she sobs out.

My eyes are wide, but my mouth silent.

"…He was supposed to confess his love for me, to say he loves me and regrets everything. He was supposed to try and save me!" Her hands clench in front of her face. This is fucked up. "…Elva only gave me a few to take the edge off, to relax me enough just to make it seem—" She stops and looks at me as if to check my reaction to what she's saying.

Holy fucking hell, Elva knew about this? She played her role well of freaking the fuck out, pretending she really thought Tina was dead. I keep holding Tina's hand, but what I want to do is slap her across the face and scream bloody murder at her. But I can't. She's crazy and crazy people do crazy things. So, instead, I sit and try to appear supportive on the outside while inside I'm terrified.

"…She gave me enough to knock me out, temporarily. Enough to give the fucking prick time to react, to worry, to tell me he wished he did *everything* differently. But he didn't!" she yells.

"Tina—he was worried. He was crying and he carried you to the car to find help…" I say, hoping that would help change her line of thinking. Deep down, I knew better.

She releases my hand and launches herself off the sofa. "He didn't do jack shit, Cal! We got in the car and he drove to the trail. I told Elva before we left where we saw the signs to the medical center. That prick had enough time to do and say anything, but what did he do? He fucking got lost halfway up the trail, got out, and had a smoke!" she yells. "Can you believe it Cal? A smoke! In the middle of an emergency. For all he knew I was dead for God sakes, but he didn't give a shit about it, did he?" Her eyes burning with fury, she continues, "…he got out to fucking smoke! So, I fucking lost it, Cal."

She fumbles in her pocket pulling out a pack of cigarettes and a lighter. "You want one?" she asks.

Fucking Ultra Capri lights, Elva smokes the same. Elva. How could she be a part of this and put us all at risk?

"So, you—"

Tina jumps in and continues her story. "I fucking knocked him out," she says, taking a long drag. She's holding the cigarette like a joint and tilting her head up to blow out the smoke calmly. "He deserved it, that fucking prick" she says as she takes another long drag.

She killed him.

"And Elva…"

Tina shoots me a look of death. Did she kill her too so there would be no witnesses? Now that she's telling me about it all, does that mean I am next? Was it her plan all along to get me to hear her confession and then kill me?

"Elva helped me drag and drop his stupid ass into a nearby ditch…" she replies as she takes the final drag and dabs the cigarette butt against the wooden table.

"Is she—"

"Is she what, Cal, dead? What am I, some type of serial killer?" she says laughing as if the thought of her taking Elva out was ridiculous.

I laugh too out of nervousness. What I want to do is cry.

"So, she's alive?"

"Of course, she's alive. What the fuck, Cal?" she says. "She's home with Tom and Flora."

She goes into the kitchen and pours herself some whiskey from the kitchen cabinet. I slowly rise up from the sofa as if to make my way towards the front door, but I stop myself and sit back down. I don't know what she is capable of. Tina looks over at me and offers me some whiskey as well. I nod. What the hell, if this is going to be my last night I might as well not feel it coming, right? She hands me a small glass, holding hers up as if to toast before she slams her whiskey.

"Ah, now that is smooth, isn't it?" she says. It's a statement more than a question.

I sling mine back remembering the way we were back at PITT. When did Tina become so cold and selfish? She does not appear to have any remorse for her actions. For taking a life of a man she supposedly loved, the man that was supposed to be the father of her child. She must have really died on this sofa and reincarnated into a total fucking psycho.

Tom and Elva are home, continuing their life with their child all the while Elva knows what Tina did to Anthony. That seems insane. And Tom, what about him? He tried to kill me himself, drugged me with the Elva's medication to make me pass out, tied me up, stashed me away multiple times. I want to ask Tina about him, but I don't have the nerve. This is all just too much. What if Joe hadn't come to pull me out of that shack? Would Tom have returned to finish me off like Tina did Anthony? Did Tina encourage Tom to do that to me? If so, why? Was Tom just trying to help them cover it up once it all went wrong and Anthony was murdered. But how? Tom was with me in the cabin—until he wasn't, but how did he know to leave? There was no reception in the cabin or out in the woods. Elva must have given him the heads up early on. He must have been with them at some point as well.

Tina holds up the whiskey, tilting her head questioningly about a second round.

I shake my head. I need to stay clear minded enough to get myself out of here.

"You weak bitch" she says as she laughs to herself before slamming back another drink. "You were always trying to fuck my brother weren't you?" she says out of the blue as she pours herself a third.

What is she talking about? When did I ever act or say anything about wanting Joe? Where is this coming from?

"You think I didn't see the way you looked at him. You thought I was so drunk that night out on the lawn I didn't know you two were seeing each other…" she says as another shot rolls down her throat.

"You're wrong Tina. I… we never--."

"Save that shit girl," she slurs, "just save it. You have been fucking my brother behind my back all these years. You thought I was an idiot. I told you he wasn't good, didn't I?"

Honestly, I wanted to, but I wasn't. Every look in his eyes gave me chills in places I couldn't say. I knew deep down I loved him when I first saw him and now I know he loves me too. Why did she care anyway? What difference did it make to her whether I was or wasn't with him?

"Tina, I have never been with Joe like that," I say, moving closer to her.

"I wanted to be *LOVED* Calista, like he loved you," so she knew he loved me then or what? "Anthony was supposed to love me, but he didn't. He fucked me sideways and left me, fucking prick. Gooooood—yeah, good—he deserved to fucking die. That bitch…" Her words slur and she's clearly drunk off her maybe seventh shot of whiskey.

How am I supposed to reason with her and explain that I did not go behind her back and sleep with her brother. I wanted to, badly, but I didn't, out of respect for her. I didn't even know he had feelings for me. She has no right to criticize me. Look what she did to Anthony!

"Was Tom in on it as well?" Anger gave me the guts to ask, as I grab the bottle of whiskey away from her and pour myself what's left of it.

"The—fuck you talking, Cal—um…"

"Did fucking Tom know about your plan to kill Anthony?" I repeat.

Tina laughs like a comic book villain as she grips the kitchen counter to hold herself up. "Tom, that bitch, would do anything for Elva. He would kiss her…her ass if she told him to." She laughs hysterically.

So that was it, they were all in on it. They all knew the pills would cause sleepiness, dizziness, all that. Of course they did, they were Elva's pills. Tina was lucky they didn't give her enough to accidentality overdose her and kill her for real.

"And me? Tom tried to drug me, was that a joke to you guys too?" I demand.

She straightens upright, coughing to clear her throat, no longer smiling or laughing. "You were just a casualty in this entire—um—thing… I knew I couldn't get you to help since you are all high and mighty Ms. Lawyer…" she says.

High and mighty?

Tina's eyes catch mine. "Yeah—all high and mighty and shit. You never cross a line Cal. You were too good for us. You were too busy for us..." she says, mumbling. "But now, you just now know too much Cal." She pulls a pistol out of a drawer next to her.

Holy shit! I take a step back, holding both hands up. "Easy there Tina, I am on your side." My voice is shaking. "You don't have to do this. Your secret is safe with me." And it's the truth. I hadn't said anything to anyone about Anthony or anything that happened.

Any thought of escaping vanishes she waves the pistol at me. She's already killed one person, what's another? I close my eyes.

BANG!

I open my eyes. I don't feel any pain so I run my hands up and down my body searching for a bullet wound. There isn't one I'm in one piece. I look to the side and see a bullet hole in the wooden table next to my leg. Jesus, that was close. I look over at Tina, her eyes filled with drunken rage. I need to get out of her line of fire. I can't keep tempting fate.

Tina advances toward me. I dodge left and right, away from the barrel of the pistol as she waves it around.

"Come on biotch—bring it!" she yells, swinging it above her head.

BANG!

This time a small piece of the ceiling falls around us.

"What the fuck is wrong with you? Are you trying to get us both killed?" I shout, as I manage to get around the kitchen island and behind her.

"I never wanted this Cal. I just wanted to be with him!" she sobs. "I can't let you—"

I grab her from behind, struggling to bring her arms down so she can't aim or fire the gun. I pull us both to the floor, her body in front of mine. I try to bring my foot high enough to kick the pistol out of her grip but miss. Tina manages to turn toward me, kicking me in the gut. My shoulder, still not fully recovered, has me screaming in pain as she brings up her leg and kicks me in the chest. *Fucking hell.* I'm gripping my shoulder in the fetal position as Tina stumbles up to her feet and points the pistol towards me.

BANG!

CHAPTER SEVENTEEN

Beep—beep—beeeeeepppp—

A light breeze caresses my hair. The sunlight warms me gently. I'm lying in a field of flowers - gardenias and tulips, my favorites. So beautiful, so intensely colorful.

Now!

I feel myself pulled out of the field, out of the flowers, away from their luscious scent.

Again!

Again!

White all around me.

Clear!

I feel a pain in my chest, and I gasp for air.

I feel air enter my lungs quickly like a burst of wind underneath and within me, like a wind tunnel.

I'm alive.

****

 The next time I open my eyes I do see flowers, but this time they're surrounding my bedside in vases. Blue, green, yellow, pink, red. They're beautiful. I try to sit up but am lightly pushed back by a small lady.

"You need to rest, dear. You've been through a lot," she says kindly.

I read her name tag, Nurse Mederin. My eyes widen. I try to speak.

"Shhh shhh, you mustn't strain yourself." She lightly fluffs my pillow behind my head. "You are in good hands now. Don't you worry," she says, gripping my hand no doubt to comfort me.

"You were involved in an… accident."

It was no accident. I may have lost my voice, but I did not lose my memory. I try to swallow making pain radiate through my throat.

"The doctors were able to successfully remove a bullet from the right side of your neck. Thankfully, the bullet just missed your carotid artery."

The nurse opens her clipboard, makes a few notes and closes it back up. She smiles at me. "Are you up for any visitors?" she asks as she walks towards the door.

I nod.

She leaves the room and returns with—*Joe*.

I think about the blocked text messages. He must have been trying to stop Tina from doing something stupid and maybe warn me as well. I watch him as he hobbles in with a bright white smile and a bouquet of red roses. He has a boot on his foot around cast leg. His eyes are swollen and red. Joy? Sorrow? Both.

"Cal-bear…" He doesn't have the words to finish. He sits in a chair next to my bed. "We almost lost you." He gently takes the hand lying on the bed and kisses it softly. His lips are soft and warm on my cold hand.

I try to speak but can't. Only a crackling sound comes out of me.

"Don't—the nurse said you need to not speak so you can heal." He kisses my hand again. "I can do the talking for now," he says as he lowers my hand back down to the bed.

"Tina didn't make it. She was messed up Cal… She wasn't in her right mind. She was obsessed with him…" Tears roll down his pale skin.

My eyes fill with salty tears. "Was—" I try to speak.

"Shhh. You were shot, Cal. Pretty bad. I could have lost both of you. They said that the bullet ricocheted from the floor and into her..." he stops and whimpers. "She was troubled."

I can't believe I survived. Or that she died, for real this time.

"Cal, there is something else," he says softly.

I raise an eyebrow.

"The police found the prescription bottle at your house..." He looks down nervously.

I try to sit up.

"The police took it into evidence. They said that Elva confessed to giving the medicine to Tina. She said Tina asked for it. Tom was a witness and agreed."

Of course, Tom agreed, he would follow Elva to the edge of the universe.

"They found the box addressed to you at your house, so they know it was sent to you," he says.

Well, that's a relief.

"But what they can't piece together yet is why it was sent to you." He shifts in his seat and lowers his voice to the point where I can barely hear him. "And also,why your prints were found on the steering wheel of the Jeep the night Anthony was killed. They found the Jeep and Anthony's body in the woods."

Jesus, what is Joe saying to me right now? The only reason my prints were in the Jeep is because I sat in it while looking for all of them. It was abandoned when I got to it.

He starts talking again. "But I explained to the police that I was with you in the cabin. That Tom had left that night while the rest were out and that I was with you the entire time thereafter. That we took a ride in the Jeep just before the incident happened with Tina," he says, smiling and gripping my hand a bit too tight and staring into my eyes. "I explained that you left to find the others initially, but I followed to help you, right before we stumbled down that cliff. Right before we were both hospitalized."

I stare back into his eyes, now less bright and more strident.

"Don't worry, love. I have us covered," he says smiling widely.

Except, Joe wasn't with me the entire time. He had left the cabin just as Tom did. I was alone in the cabin for a long time before I ventured out to find the others. The footsteps in the snow were there before I ever stepped foot outside. I was alone then, and suddenly I feel alone now.

CHAPTER EIGHTEEN

It was supposed to be easy. We were just going to get rid of him. No one else was supposed to get hurt. We planned it well. Elva even agreed to give her medication to Tina to make it look like she was dead or nearly dead. Elva said she used to take it before bed. Something about easing her breath in between inhales, slowing the heart down a little to relax. It was perfect.

Tina only took a few, and it seemed to have worked quickly. We had to time it well so that when Cal came down the stairs she would be surprised, and Tina would look dead. We knew Cal would be questioning everything from the hike earlier in the day. Tina had to make it look like she was weak, like she couldn't stand up on her own two feet. She gave one hell of a performance too.

I sent those messages from my cell phone. I blocked the number to make sure Cal didn't know they were from me at the time. I had to send one to Tina's phone too so it would look like I was trying to get in touch with both of them. You know, to create a sense of urgency. I didn't know the cell reception would be so bad, but it seems like it worked in my favor.

The plan was to have Cal stay back at the cabin while Anthony and Elva took Tina to seek medical assistance. It was a gamble whether Cal would actually stay back in the cabin, but it made sense for her to so she could call for help if the phones started working again. I knew they wouldn't because I disabled the

cabins signal amplifier and WI-FI when everyone was out on the balcony the night before.

Tom was supposed to wait for me outside when the others left to go meet up with them and help us get rid of Anthony's body. He wasn't where he was supposed to be when I got back to the cabin. Instead, he'd gone back inside and started drinking. He was pathetic. I watched Cal try to start the Jag. Luckily, I'd disconnected the car's battery just in case, otherwise the entire plan would have been ruined. While she was outside, I went inside to wake up Tom and get him up to finish the job. Cal returned too soon, so I pushed him out onto the roof outside of Cal's bedroom window and told him to wait for me.

I covered her mouth and dragged her into the closet, not to scare her, but to make it look like I was shielding her. I wanted her to be suspicious of Tom but never me. When I looked around I saw Tom left the cabin. That idiot never follows instructions, so I had to go after him to make sure he was doing what he was supposed to.

Unfortunately, that left Cal alone in the house again and gave her the opportunity to come search for us. I did not take that into account. Especially since I had revealed to her that I was there. That was definitely not a part of the plan. When I saw Cal find

the Jeep I knew we had run out of time. We had to leave Anthony behind. Tina didn't want to, but I told her she had to. I hit him over the head with a log, knocking him into the ditch. It worked out perfectly since he broke his neck when he fell in. I think that's what really killed him and not the log I hit him with. Poor guy. Tina screamed when I hit Anthony. She really shouldn't have done that, especially since she'd hit him with a log in the back right before. Did she have second thoughts about killing him? Maybe. But I was only doing what a good big brother would do, protecting my sister, right?

Anyway, Cal was too involved at that point, especially when she stumbled on Anthony's body. It would have been easier if she'd stayed back at the cabin like a good girl. You know, like she was instructed to do.

I didn't want to hurt her, I just wanted to get her out of harm's way for a little while. It wasn't that cold outside; she would have been fine in the ditch for a little while. She sure had some fight in her, even with her shoulder being injured. I didn't want that to happen to her.

I told Tom to get her and put her in the one-room cabin in the woods, at least it was out of the elements. That way she could settle down a bit. Give us time to figure out what to do with the body and a good story for what she'd seen. It was a little difficult getting Tom on track, he was constantly chasing after Elva,

making sure she was okay. But he did well giving Cal a few of those pills. I was impressed when he dissolved them in the water.

I couldn't even tell they were in there. The water looked very clear.

But you know what bothered me the most? I felt like Cal was doubting me, like I might be the bad guy. So, naturally, I came to her rescue like a hero. I saved her from Tom, that villain. Man was she excited when she saw me. I wanted to kiss her then, but I thought I would wait a little bit, make it more dramatic. I didn't plan to take that fall down the hill and shatter my leg. That wrecked me. The only good thing that came from it was her being right next to me. She trusted me then. Especially when I told her I loved her. She was eating out of the palm of my hand.

I asked the nurse to not release any information about me, no matter who asked. I needed to make sure I could meet with Tina first. I reminded her that I put the gun in the kitchen drawer and told her that we needed to get Cal back to the cabin to get rid of her before she told the cops everything she knew. I was sad but she just knew too much.

I made sure Tom mailed the pills to Cal's house before she got back home. I knew that if the cops found them at her place, they'd be suspicious of her. I told Tina maybe it was in our best interest to pin it all on Cal. Make her look like the one with a problem. It wouldn't be unreasonable for the cops to think that she stole the medicine from Elva. She's been so isolated, working all the time, no social life, the cops would believe it. I made sure Anthony had some in his system too before Tina took the first hit, you know to ease the pain, so it really covered all our bases.

When I told Elva to email Cal asking her to go back to the cabin, she was reluctant. "Hasn't this gone far enough?" she said.

And that's when I knew we could no longer rely on her. I had to access her account and send the damn email myself. So unnecessary. Just like clockwork, when Cal got the message she left straight for the cabin, which gave me plenty of time to enter her house, pet Mr. Whiskers, and take back the note in the package, leaving the pills behind.

Then Tina got so emotional. She always messes things up. She was sloppy when she had a few drinks, which wasn't a part of the plan either. My little sister was not supposed to be the one who ended up dead. Unfortunately, it was her and I reverted to Plan B. I had to make sure Cal and I were on the same page. She was already in love with me, held a steady job, and believed I was a hero. She would back me up no matter what, right? Plus, her best friend that just died was my sister. I'm in mourning too.

I also had to blackmail Tom and tell him that if he and Elva didn't fess up to giving Tina access to the pills I would tell everyone that Flora was really mine. Tom agreed and paid me to keep it quiet. I didn't care about Elva. I needed the money. I'd dropped out of college ages ago and hadn't been able to keep a 9 to 5 job. Poor Tom couldn't have his own children. I knew that somehow helping them would work in my favor and it did just four years later. Sometimes I cannot believe how smart I am.

Anyway, Tina was already gone, no sense of pinning it all on Cal now, right?

In the end, I'm glad that even with this tragic ending I was able to help my sister. I know she appreciates it even if she isn't around to see it. Anthony was a bad guy, he treated her poorly. Cal and I can name our first daughter after her.

Acknowledgements

A special thanks to my husband, Matt, and my mom, Mirjana, for all of their love and support during this process. This book wouldn't exist without either of you. Thank you to my cuddly little girl, Bambi, for the hours we spent together, day and night, writing, rewriting, editing, formatting, and self-publishing this novel to make it unique and our own.

To all the readers: I am *beyond* excited to share my first novel with you. I appreciate the time you took from your busy lives to pick up and read my book. Thank you from the bottom of my heart, I feel blessed and grateful for this opportunity.